Deck the Shops

Kristen Grafton

Cottage House Publishing

For my family who always made Christmas magical:
No matter how many Christmas romance movies we watch with the same
plot,
I'll always want to watch more with you.

1

Emily

Emily pulled the last batch of gingerbread cookies out of the oven and smiled: they were perfectly baked. It was still a little early for gingerbread by the standards of some—after all, Thanksgiving was just days ago—but Emily felt it was never too early for a perfectly soft, chewy gingerbread cookie with icing.

While she waited for them to cool before icing them, she turned her attention to the drinks she had been preparing. She'd spent a lot of time getting the recipes just right, but she felt she'd finally done it. Surely her grandparents would have to see her reasoning now.

She grabbed one of the wooden plates with the poinsettias carved into the edges and laid out a few sugar cookies and fresh gingerbread. She knew Grandpa liked the more traditional sugar cookies, but Grandma never could turn away a fresh gingerbread cookie. On her two drink trays, she inserted the miniature glasses, each one a different Christmasy drink. She checked her watch and found that the bakery didn't open for another fifteen minutes. Perfect.

Balancing a cookie tray on one arm, she grabbed a drink tray in each hand and carefully pushed through the swinging door to the main room. Her grandparents were sitting at a table together, her grandfather reading the morning paper and her grandmother going over the inventory lists as they always did on Monday mornings. Since opening the bakery together, they'd never missed a Monday morning together. Even if one of them was sick, they still had breakfast together. It was sweet, and Emily considered herself fortunate to have grown up around that kind of commitment to both marriage and to business.

"Okay," Emily said with a smile. "Here's what I've been working on."

She laid out each of the drink trays in front of her grandparents and set the cookies between the three of them. She noticed the icing was dripping a little bit on the gingerbread since they were still so warm, but she knew it wouldn't matter. If anything, her grandmother liked them better that way.

"It looks lovely," her grandmother said with a smile. She was that kind of older woman who had a lot of lines on her face, but it almost made her more beautiful because they were lines that spoke of frequent smiling in life. "Ooh, you know I can't resist these," she said as she snagged a cookie.

"What is this, exactly?" her grandfather asked. He was the tougher nut to crack, but she had to try.

"Well," Emily said, "obviously I made your favorite cookies, but here's my idea: Christmas drink flights. The first is peppermint hot chocolate, the second is a gingerbread chai tea latte, the third is a white chocolate mocha coffee, and the fourth is an eggnog matcha latte made with oat milk."

Her grandfather furrowed his brow and pushed his glasses a little higher up on his face. When Emily was a child, she had often thought it funny how much her grandfather resembled Santa Claus. He had sported the thick white beard her entire life, and decades of running a bakery showed on his waistline. There was a time when Emily even thought he might be Santa Claus because he seemed so jolly and magical, but she also knew that he could be tough and stubborn, and while that had served him well in many areas of his life—his time in the army, his persistence to maintain the bakery during the recession, and his successful fight against cancer years ago—it also meant that it was very difficult to change his mind.

"I don't know," he said, "it seems like it's a bit much. Coffee is just coffee."

"Not anymore, Grandpa," Emily said. "Most people don't like black coffee. And besides, these are seasonal. They're festive."

"Eh, every coffee chain sells stuff like this."

"Because they sell."

"It just feels gimmicky to me."

"Grandpa, you haven't even tasted them."

He wasn't an unreasonable man, so that did give him pause. Her grandmother had already sampled the gingerbread chai and the peppermint hot cocoa and seemed pleased with both. Emily knew her grandmother wouldn't try the eggnog matcha—both of her grandparents hated matcha because they thought it tasted like grass—but each of them picked up the white chocolate mocha at the same time and tasted. They both seemed pleased, and while Emily was pretty sure that her grandmother would find the drink too sweet, she knew her grandfather was a sucker for anything involving white chocolate.

"This tastes good," he said after a while, and Emily felt like maybe he was reluctant to admit it. "But it's not what we do. We sell baked goods, not coffee."

"But there's no reason why we can't do both," Emily said. "Coffee and desserts go together perfectly."

"We don't have the equipment to make these kinds of drinks regularly."

"We could buy the equipment."

"We don't have the money for that," her grandmother added.

"It would be an investment. The coffee sales would more than cover the cost over time."

Her grandfather harrumphed and crossed his arms. Emily knew that was a bad sign. "And why a flight? Why not serve normal sized drinks?"

"Well, we would sell full-sized versions, too, but this is a fun way for people to find out what they like or for friends or couples to share. Flights are big money makers. Usually, they result in another sale of a full-sized drink."

"Eh, it's too cutesy," he said. "The bakery is classic. That's why it's been successful all this time."

"I know, but the profit margin is getting slimmer every year."

He sat forward. "We're in the black."

"Of course, but the time to act is not when you're in the red. It's now so that you never end up there."

He grabbed a sugar cookie and munched on it. "Sweet pea," he began, and Emily knew she was cooked anytime he broke out that nickname. "I know you're just trying to help, but your grandmother and I have been running this bakery for a long time, and it's successful. What we do works because we're classic. If you get swept up in the trends, you lose the heart, and that's what we've got here is heart."

"You know I'm not trying to take away the heart of the bakery."

Her grandmother smiled. "I think what your grandfather is trying to say is that you shouldn't worry too much over a problem that isn't yours to bear."

Emily looked around the bakery. It was small with a seating area for maybe twelve people, but it was homey and always had been. Growing up, Emily had felt she had spent more time here than at home. Both of her parents had worked, so her grandmother had always picked her up from school, and she'd do her homework while sitting at the counter. When her parents retired to Florida, something just hadn't sat right with Emily about leaving the bakery and this town. It was home.

Her grandmother was wrong that it wasn't her problem to bear. This bakery meant everything to her.

Emily sighed. "I just want to feel like I'm doing something that matters here. I've been the general manager for two years, and I just want to help. You both know how much Sweet Treats means to me."

"We know, honey," her grandmother said, "but don't worry. We're doing just fine."

"And it's time to open," her grandfather said as he pushed himself up from the table and grabbed another cookie. "Would you clear this table, sweet pea? I'm going to check on the pies."

He disappeared into the kitchen, and Emily's grandmother smiled at her and gave her arm a squeeze. "You're doing a great job. Just keep doing what you're doing."

But that was exactly it, wasn't it? Emily didn't want to just keep doing exactly what she was doing. She wanted to do more.

2

Michael

Michael checked his watch for the third time in the last twenty minutes that he'd been sitting outside of the office conference room before grabbing the copy of *A Tale of Two Cities* he had tucked into his briefcase that morning. Sure, he'd read it before, and maybe he could have chosen a more relaxing book rather than one set during the French Revolution, but it was one of his favorites, and something about the winter season always put him in the mood for Charles Dickens.

His boss was running late. Again. He'd gotten used to that over the ten years that he'd worked for this firm, and Michael didn't usually mind because he always had a book on him and genuinely enjoyed reading. But today, Michael was feeling more and more tense as the minutes ticked by. Today was his performance review, and he'd been in line for a promotion for many months now. Though nothing had been confirmed, there were rumors that Alex Hancock had accepted an offer from a rival firm and was leaving in the new year, which meant that Michael's natural next step was falling into his lap.

His phone rang, rudely interrupting his immersion in Dickens's world, but when he saw Darren Moore's name on his phone, his anger quickly faded, and he answered the call.

"Darren! How's it going?"

"Good, man, how about you?" Darren said.

Darren had been Michael's college roommate at Northwestern, and they'd kept in touch over the years. They hadn't seen each other in person for a while, but they tried to call each other every so often. Darren had been one of the best parts of Michael's time at Northwestern. They had been fast friends.

"Just working," Michael said.

"I'm not catching you at a bad time, am I?'

Michael looked across the hall at the conference room door. He didn't see any movement. "No, waiting for a meeting with my boss."

"Uh oh," Darren said with a laugh. "Not getting fired, are you?"

Michael laughed, too. "Of course not." He checked to see if anyone was nearby and would overhear, but he found that he was alone. "Actually, I think I might be getting a promotion. This guy just quit and moved to another investment firm, and I've been working my tail off."

"I'm sure you'll get it. They'd be idiots not to give it to you."

Michael smiled. Darren was the best for pep talks. "I hope you're right. I've put in a ton of extra hours lately, and all of my investments are doing well. But it's a big firm, you know? Anything could happen."

"Well, once you get the promotion and can take a break, you should try to take a vacation and relax."

"I don't take breaks."

He laughed. "That's kind of my point, man. You've been working too hard."

"Working hard is a good thing, you know. That's how you get the promotions. Besides, if I get the promotion, that's the time to speed up, not slow down."

"So what are you going to do? Work straight through the holidays?"

Michael shrugged though he knew that Darren couldn't see him. "I've done it before. Not really a point in sitting home alone."

The truth was that Michael hadn't really celebrated the holidays in a while. He didn't have family around anymore, and unless he happened to be dating someone when the holidays rolled around, he mostly didn't bother. It wasn't that he hated Christmas or anything—Michael wasn't a Scrooge or a Grinch despite accusations that had been leveled at him by former girlfriends, friends, and coworkers—but he just really didn't see the point if it would just be him.

"What if you spent the holidays with me and my family?" Darren offered, and it wasn't the first time he had. "Tennessee is beautiful this time of year, and our town does a whole Christmas festival. It's a lot of fun."

Darren had grown up in Tennessee, and when they'd graduated, he'd moved right back to his hometown. It had never made sense to Michael. He had lived in Chicago pretty much his whole life, but he didn't love it. In fact, he didn't really think that was a normal thing. He wondered how someone could like a place so much you'd move back as an adult.

"I appreciate it, but if I get this promotion, I'll have a lot on my plate here. It would be a bad time to leave Chicago."

"You always say it's a bad time to leave Chicago."

"It's always true."

"Well, consider it a standing invitation. And whatever you do, try to relax and enjoy the holidays at least a little bit."

Michael laughed. "I'll try."

The conference room door opened, and his coworker Eric walked past him. Eric got on Michael's nerves. He was always sucking up to the boss while trying to make everyone else look bad so that he looked better by comparison. Michael hated the type. He believed in getting ahead based on your own merits, not based on putting others down.

"Michael," Eric said, "good to see you. Same old, same old, huh?"

"Darren, I've got to go," Michael said, ignoring Eric. "Talk to you later." He hung up and forced a smile. "Eric."

"Oh, I'm sorry, were you waiting to meet with Ron? My bad, we just got to talking and lost track of time."

Yet another thing about Eric that bothered Michael: he was always trying to act like he was best buddies with their boss Ron.

"No problem," Michael said as he stood and buttoned his suit jacket. "I don't mind waiting."

"Good, good," he said with a smile that made Michael grimace. "Well, I'll let you get to it."

Eric walked off, and Michael forced himself to take a deep breath before shoving his book back into his briefcase and walking through the door. Ron always liked to have meetings in the conference room rather than his own office because he liked the open space. Honestly, Michael never really minded it. It was less intimidating to sit around a table together rather than on opposite sides of a desk. Conversations here felt more like a collaboration rather than an interrogation.

"Michael, good to see you," Ron said. "Have a seat."

Michael sat down two chairs away from Ron—close enough to show that he was confident and not intimidated but not so close that it was awkward.

Ron continued, "Well, I'm sure you've heard the rumors about Hancock moving to Eastern Elite Investments." Michael nodded. "Well, they are true. His last day will be December tenth. Management has done a lot of thinking about the situation, and your name has come up a lot as someone we can always depend on."

Michael smiled. "I'm happy to hear that. You know Rothstein Investments is very important to me."

"It shows. You've worked here for many years now. I remember when I hired you. I knew then that you showed a lot of promise."

"Thank you, sir."

"It's nice to know that we have employees like you that are loyal to the company."

Michael could read between the lines: taking a job offer from Eastern Elite Investments was not very loyal. But almost Michael's entire career had been with Rothstein. He'd been the epitome of loyal, and it was finally going to pay off.

Ron continued, "So in this time of transition as we look for Hancock's replacement, we need to know that we can rely on people like you."

"Of course, sir," Michael said. "I'm here for whatever you need."

"That's good to hear. You've got a lot of knowledge about Rothstein that is hard to replicate. Your experience here is invaluable. That's why we'd like you to come alongside Connors and help him as he steps into Hancock's role."

Michael felt the blood in his ears pounding, and suddenly, he felt too warm for his jacket. "Excuse me? Eric Connors?"

"Yes, well, he's only worked here for a little while, so he just doesn't have the background knowledge that you have about Rothstein. We'd love it if you could help him prepare for this new role."

"You want me to train Eric to replace Alex?"

"I guess you could put it that way, yes."

Michael knew he probably shouldn't say what he was about to say, but it felt as if he couldn't stop the words before they bubbled out. "I thought I was going to get that job."

Ron looked a bit confused. "Don't get me wrong, Anderson, you're a valuable part of Rothstein, but that's just it. You're extremely valuable in your existing position. We don't know what we'd do without you."

"But you want me to tell Eric everything I know because I have more experience here than him? Doesn't that make me more qualified for the role? I've been doing a lot of research, sir, and I think I can help Rothstein Investments get to the next level. I've got some ideas, and—"

Ron held up his hands to stop Michael. "I appreciate the effort, but we've got to think of the big picture here. Eric is a really innovative thinker. He's young and hungry, and we think he's got what it takes, but he's inexperienced. He could learn so much from you."

Michael didn't try to stop the scoffing noise that rose up in his throat. "Eric's worked here for 14 months. He's barely out of college. I've been here ten years. I've put in so much overtime, I've worked extra hours, I've come in on holidays, and you want me to train someone to take a promotion I should have gotten?"

"Now Mr. Anderson—"

"I quit," Michael said without thinking, and once the words were out, he was filled with a mixture of confidence and fear.

"You what?"

Michael stood, buttoned his coat, and grabbed his briefcase. "Consider this my resignation. I am grateful for my time at Rothstein, but I think it's time that I move on."

"I'm not sure you know what you're doing," Ron said, the tone of his voice issuing a warning.

"I'll have my office cleaned out by the end of the day."

And with that, Michael turned on his heel and walked out of the office. He felt his heart racing, and part of him wanted to turn right around and beg Ron to forget everything he'd just said, but then he thought about training Eric and his pretentious face for the job he should have gotten, and that mental image was enough to make him keep walking.

He thought back on the ten years he'd spent at Rothstein, and what had been the point? His job was boring, and he'd never really liked it, but he was good at it. The one light at the end of the tunnel was that he was going to get this promotion, but for what? Darren had been right. A promotion meant more hours, more paperwork, and less of anything he actually enjoyed. He was good at his job, but there was no point staying at a job he hated if he wasn't even going to be appreciated or recognized for his hard work. Part of the reason Michael was a good investment banker was that he never took risks, but maybe this was a worthwhile risk.

He rounded the corner to his office, and before he began packing up his stuff, he sat at his computer and searched for flights to Tennessee.

3

Emily

Friday mornings were Emily's favorite at the bakery. They were busy enough that she never got bored but not so busy that she went home exhausted at the end of the day. Friday was also the day that Sweet Treats saw the most tourists passing through. Bells wasn't too far from Memphis or even Nashville, but it was quiet and picturesque, so people who wanted to enjoy the fall or winter seasons in the country often sought out places like Bells.

Emily had her hands full making sure she made everything that they would need for the weekend. Her grandparents liked to be prepared in case a big rush came in. It almost never did, except around Christmas.

She'd made enough snickerdoodle cookies and gingerbread to last the weekend, and if she found she needed an extra batch, those didn't take long to make. There weren't enough sugar cookies, but honestly, a bakery could never have enough sugar cookies. Her focus today would have to be cakes. They'd sold out of the few they'd made, and though cake wasn't exactly Sweet Treats' biggest seller, she knew her grandfather would be upset if they didn't have any. It was quiet in the storefront, so it seemed like a good time to step into the back and make some, but just as she was heading through the swinging door, the bell above the front door jingled, and Emily had a customer.

The first thing Emily thought about the man who walked in was that he was very handsome, and she felt a little silly that that was her first thought. She assumed he was a tourist because his navy suit made him a little overdressed for the small town life. He had a sharp jawline, and his sandy hair had just enough body to betray that he probably put some effort into styling it. But he definitely looked a little out of place and like he didn't really know how he had found himself in a small town bakery.

"Hello," Emily said. "Can I help you find something?"

He smiled. "I'm not really sure what I'm looking for."

Emily furrowed her eyebrows. "You don't know what kind of dessert you like?"

"Oh, I know what kind of dessert I like. That's easily a chocolate cream pie. But I'm not trying to buy something for myself. I'm visiting a friend, and I want to bring him something."

"And you don't know what kind of dessert he likes?"

He shook his head. "He's a college friend. Haven't seen him in a while."

"Any chance I know him?" When he gave her a strange look, Emily added, "It's a small town. Chances are he's a regular customer of mine."

His face betrayed some skepticism, but he relented with a sigh. "Darren Moore."

Emily nodded in recognition. "He's never come in here and not ordered snickerdoodles."

"Well, in that case, give me a dozen."

"And his wife absolutely adores our coconut cream pie."

"Then I guess I better get one of those, too."

"And their kids go nuts for our holiday sugar cookies."

He folded his arms. "I'm starting to wonder if you really know your clients this well or if you're just an excellent saleswoman."

Emily smiled sweetly. "I guess you'll never know."

"Then you better give me a pie and some sugar cookies."

Emily nodded and started boxing the baked goods. "Can I interest you in any coffee while you're here? We have some special seasonal blends for the holidays."

"Oh no, I don't really go for all that frilly stuff."

Emily scoffed. "Frilly?"

"Sure, I mean, what's wrong with just a black coffee anymore?"

"Nothing's wrong with it, but don't you ever want something different?"

"Not really," he said. "It's traditional. Tried and true."

"A peppermint stick never hurt anyone, you know."

"I beg to differ. As a kid, I licked a candy cane until it became sharp, and I cut the inside of my mouth."

"That sounds like user error."

He smiled. "I'll take a black coffee."

Emily forced a smile. "You got it. $21.50."

"For all that?" he asked as he pulled out his wallet. "I was expecting this to hurt more than it does."

"I take it you're from the city."

"What makes you say that?"

"You're expecting a bakery to rip you off. Baked goods don't cost that much to make. Anyone charging a high markup is just in it to take your money."

"That's kind of cynical, don't you think?"

"Says the guy expecting a bakery to bleed him dry."

He smirked a little, and Emily felt confident that she had won. She handed him his card and the box, and he seemed to want to say more but struggled with what to say.

Emily beat him to it: "Tell Darren and Renee I said hello. Enjoy your black coffee."

"Thanks, I think."

As he walked out, Emily smiled to herself. She knew she'd hear about this visitor from Renee later. She couldn't wait to hear her thoughts on the uptight city interloper. What on earth was he doing in Bells? He didn't seem to fit in.

Still, he hadn't struck her the way other city people did who passed through Bells. Most were judgmental or in far too much of a hurry. This man had seemed calm and willing to roll with the punches of small town life. He'd been—well, he'd been charming, though Emily tried not to notice. People like him never stayed in a slow place like Bells for long.

4

Michael

Michael left the quaint little bakery with its opinionated baker and started walking back toward where he had parked his rental car. He was still fighting conflicting feelings. On the one hand, he felt so relaxed walking through the center of this cute little downtown holding a box of baked goods, soon to see his best friend whom he hadn't seen in far too long. On the other, he was paralyzed by fear and anxiety. Was quitting the right call? Shouldn't he be searching for a new job? But he just kept reminding himself that it was too close to Christmas to job hunt anyway. Any applications he submitted now wouldn't be reviewed until January, so he might as well relax.

And he smiled when he thought about the woman running the bakery. She was—what was she, exactly? She'd made him laugh, and while she had questionable beliefs about coffee, he found her kind of charming in a small town kind of way. She was the kind of quirky townsperson Michael only ever read about in books or saw in movies. He was somewhat bemused to find that people like her were real.

He was about to cross the street to his car when he noticed a little bookshop called "Something Worth Reading," and Michael couldn't resist the urge to go in when he saw it. Michael had loved bookstores since he was a little kid. His mom used to take him at least once a month so that he could pick out a new book. It was like a treasure hunt, finding just the right story. He usually tore through the books in less than a week, and then he would rent whatever his local library would let him until the next month when he got to find a new treasure.

When Darren first got married and he and Renee had kids, Michael had sent them some children's books as a gift. He'd done that for a couple of years after that on the kids' birthdays, but he'd stopped doing it years ago, though he couldn't remember why. Maybe he'd thought he was too busy or maybe he just lost touch. That changed starting now, he decided.

Michael walked into the bookstore, breathed in deeply, and immediately smiled. It had that old indie bookstore smell that he loved so much—the smell of aged paper and wooden shelves and just a little bit of dust. It wasn't huge compared to a big chain bookstore, but it was bigger than most indie bookstores he saw these days. He walked over to the elderly woman who was running the register and smiled.

"Welcome," she said when she noticed him. "Are you visiting Bells?"

Michael laughed. "Is it that obvious?"

She smiled and glanced down at his expensive suit and shiny oxfords, but she said, "I've lived here a long time. I don't often see people I don't know. Can I help you find anything?"

He nodded. "I'm visiting my best friend and his family, but don't want to show up empty handed. I'd like to surprise his kids with some books. Where is your kids section?"

"Follow me," she said as she shuffled out in front of him.

"I love the name of the bookstore, by the way," Michael said. "'Something Worth Reading?' From the Benjamin Franklin quote?"

She turned around and smiled wide. "Why yes. 'Either write something worth reading or do something worth writing.' I've always loved that quote."

"Me, too."

"Big history buff?"

Michael shook his head. "Not really, but I'm a big reader."

She stopped in front of the children's section and put both hands on her hips. "Okay, what's your all-time favorite book? I can tell a lot about a person based on their favorite book."

"Now I'm a little intimidated."

She raised an eyebrow. "Well?"

"*The Adventures of Huckleberry Finn.*"

She smiled and closed her eyes. "Ah, a classic. You're old school, traditional, but you love a good adventure and believe in what's right."

"You can decide all that based on my favorite book?"

"Of course. Well, here's the children's section. What ages are the kids?"

"Two boys, eleven and nine."

She plucked a book off the shelf. "Can't go wrong with *Percy Jackson*. So many boys love it. Have they read it?"

"I don't know. I haven't seen them in a while."

"Well, if they've read the first one, just bring it back, and we can exchange it for whichever book in the series they're on." She handed him the book and pointed at a shelf behind her. "And for the younger, anything on this shelf should work. Take your time. I'll ring you up at the front when you're ready."

Michael glanced at the books on the designated shelf. He was woefully ignorant of children's books and had no idea what Darren's kids might like. He wondered if maybe he should just close his eyes and pick one. Suddenly he noticed a cover with a dragon, and he had a faint recollection that Darren's kids like dragon stories, so he grabbed that one and hoped he was right.

He took his time walking back to the front, taking a moment to eye some of the other shelves. This woman had everything. Her shelves were lined with classics, new releases, bestsellers, local authors, leather bound special editions, worn and used paperbacks, and even some reference books. He wondered what it must have taken to amass a collection like this: how much time and money she must have invested. And frankly, how she turned a profit. Since he had come in, he was the only customer to be seen.

Michael's phone buzzed in his pocket, and when he checked his watch, he saw that it was later in the day than he thought, and he was late getting over to Darren's. In fact, it was Darren who was calling, no doubt to find out where he was. Regretfully, he made his way to the register, promising himself he'd come back to this shop before this trip was over.

"Excellent choice," the woman said when she saw the dragon cover.

"You think so?"

She nodded emphatically. "Definitely. A very popular one." She glanced down at the box from Sweet Treats still tucked under his arm as Michael passed her his credit card. "I see you stopped by Sweet Treats already. They have the best pastries and cookies in town."

"Glad to hear it. The woman behind the counter did some serious upselling."

"Ah, Emily. Yes, she drives a hard bargain."

"So I found out. I think she could sell cocoa to Santa himself."

The woman nodded again bemusedly, rolling the books in some tissue paper and sliding them into a brown paper bag with handles embossed with the bookstore logo. "Enjoy your books and your pastries," she said, handing the bag over to Michael. "I'm having a sale this weekend if you'd like to stop by again."

"I'm so glad you said something. I will definitely be back."

Michael walked out of the bookstore feeling like himself for the first time in a while. Just like when he was a child, the bookstore had healed something that he hadn't even realized was broken. More and more, he was thinking that this trip was exactly what he needed.

5

Emily

O nce the cupcakes were fully iced and decorated, Emily arranged them on a platter and spun around looking for the edible glitter. Her grandfather hated the stuff, but Emily knew it was perfect for what she was trying to do. She sprinkled only a tiny bit on each cupcake and smiled when she saw how they looked. She'd decorated seven cupcakes, each one modeled after a specific holiday, and she was so proud of them. After the holiday drink flight fiasco, she hadn't thought her grandparents would entertain any more of ideas, but her grandmother had been willing to listen to her cupcake idea.

Sweet Treats didn't serve cupcakes, and even as a child, Emily had thought that was strange. What bakery didn't serve cupcakes? Cake could be ordered by the slice, by the cake size, or custom for special events like weddings or birthday parties, but Emily couldn't recall a single time this bakery had served cupcakes. This was a risky presentation, but that's what Emily was all about.

Emily took the tray out to the storefront and sat at a booth with her grandmother.

"These are very cute, Emily," her grandmother said. "Oh, I love the little Christmas tree on this one. And the cupid's bow on that pink one is just darling."

"I did one for every major holiday. Fireworks for July 4th, an egg for Easter, a pumpkin for Halloween, a cornucopia for Thanksgiving, and a four leaf clover for St. Patrick's Day. And each one is a different flavor that matches the time of year. The Christmas one has peppermint icing, the Halloween one is pumpkin with cream cheese icing."

"They're absolutely adorable, but didn't these take a while to ice?"

Emily shook her head. "Once you've got the design down, it's really easy to replicate. I could teach you."

Her grandmother waved her hands. "Oh no, I don't think I'd be any good at that."

Emily took a deep breath and tried to shake off the fear of history repeating itself. "I think these would be fun to sell year-round. We could always stock cupcakes, but around the holidays, we can make these specialty cupcakes. We could even charge just a little bit more for them since they're more than just plain icing without decoration. It would be a fun incentive for people to visit the bakery more often."

Before her grandmother could answer, her grandfather returned from the post office errand he'd set out on. *Drat,* Emily thought. She was hoping she could convince her grandmother that this was a good idea before he got back and shot it down.

"Stamps went up again," he said.

"Look, honey," her grandmother said, "Emily made cupcakes."

Grandpa came over to the booth and sat across from Emily and his wife and inspected them. "They're cute. May I?" he gestured at the Valentine's cupcake, and Emily nodded. She was grateful he had chosen that one because it was a devil's food cupcake with raspberry filling, and her grandfather loved raspberries.

"It's delicious," he said after a few moments.

"I thought we could sell them."

His face immediately fell. "Emily, I thought we talked about this."

"We talked about my drink flight, not about cupcakes."

"I've told you before, we don't do cupcakes."

"But it doesn't make any sense. All bakeries sell cupcakes."

He settled into the booth, pushing his glasses up his nose and folding his arms. "Sweet Treats isn't just any bakery."

"I know that, but—"

"It's gimmicky."

"But kids love them."

"They can buy a slice of cake."

"But kids don't want a slice of cake. They want a cupcake. Besides, we could sell these cute holiday designs for parties."

"It feels like a money grab. I just don't like it."

"Honey," Grandma said, "maybe it's not such a bad idea."

"Eleanor, we've succeeded because we've remained traditional. All this cutesy stuff looks like a fad or something. It won't last."

Before Emily could answer, Mayor Rayburn walked into the shop, tinkling the little bell above the door. "Good morning!"

"Laura," Grandma said. "Lovely to see you."

"I'm here to drop off the entry forms for this year's Deck the Shops competition."

Deck the Shops, a play on words of the Christmas song "Deck the Halls," was a Bells, Tennessee tradition and had been for the last twenty years or so. It was a friendly competition for the local businesses. Each business would enter and do some kind of pop-up event that was holiday themed and compete for the most interest and sales. The winning business got a very small cash prize, but that wasn't why most businesses entered. There were bragging rights to be earned as the business with "Most Holiday

Spirit," and most businesses saw that as the far more important prize. Sweet Treats had won more than any other business in town.

Her grandfather took a form and smiled. "Of course we're entering. Got a title to protect." He was very proud of his record, with seven wins over the last twenty years, including being the current reigning champion.

Suddenly, Emily sat up a little straighter. Deck the Shops just might be the solution to her problem.

"Wait, I have an idea," she said to her grandparents. "Let me run our Deck the Shops event this year."

Grandma said, "It's a lot of work, dear."

"I know, but hear me out. I'll run an event that incorporates all of my ideas. If people like the ideas and we win, then maybe we can make some additions to our menu. If it doesn't work, then I'll let it go."

"Ooh," Mayor Rayburn said, "What an exciting proposition."

Her grandmother's crooked smile was a touch wry, and Emily knew she had won her over. She looked across the booth at her grandfather whose face still looked impressively skeptical with his eyes looking over his glasses and his eyebrows furrowed. But there was something about the sparkle in his eyes—it was almost excitement. Very little could beat out his love of winning.

He jutted out his hand. "Deal."

Emily shook it and snatched up the entry form he slid across the table as her grandmother and Mayor Rayburn clapped. Emily was elated that she finally had the chance to prove herself, but she also knew that she couldn't blow this opportunity or her grandfather would never want to hear another one of her ideas ever again. She had to win.

6

Michael

Michael pulled into Darren's driveway and chuckled to himself when he saw the house. There were more Christmas decorations than seemed physically possible all over the house and crammed all across the lawn. There were inflatable penguins, candy canes everywhere, mismatched lights across every eave and fence, and a lighted life-sized nativity by the garage. It was far more than Michael ever would have used on his own house, and he couldn't help but think that it looked a little tacky to have so many different decorations. Still, something about it made him smile. He thought that it seemed warm and familial. His parents always hired a company to decorate the house, so everything was perfect with only white lights arranged symmetrically and exactly. This chaos he was looking at betrayed the chaos of a happy family with kids, and there was something endearing about that.

By the time he grabbed his luggage from the backseat, Darren had walked out of his front door with a big smile. "You made it."

Before Michael could answer, Darren's kids burst out the door behind him only half-wearing jackets as Darren's wife trailed behind them yelling half-hearted pleas for them to button their coats. Both kids made a beeline for a pile of snow in the front yard and set about making a snowman. Michael couldn't help but laugh.

"Sorry," Renee said with a sheepish smile. "I didn't know you were out here."

Michael was still laughing. "No problem. They're cute."

Darren gave Michael a hug, and Renee smiled as she pulled her coat tighter around her. "It's good to see you, man," Darren said.

"You, too," Michael said. He pulled the paper bag from Something Worth Reading from the passenger seat and followed Darren and Renee inside, hoisting his other bags over his shoulder.

"Would you like some coffee?" Renee asked.

"Please," Michael said and handed the bag to Darren. "Here, these are for the kids. I stopped at that bookstore downtown."

Darren laughed and handed the bag to Renee. "I'm not surprised. You never could resist a bookstore." He turned to Renee. "In college, I don't think I ever saw this guy without a book. When we were roommates, I was convinced that he was lying about being a finance major. As often as he read, I figured he had to have been an English major."

Renee smiled. "Really? Michael, who is your favorite author? I'm a bit of a reader myself."

"Definitely Charles Dickens."

"He's lovely. I've always been partial to Agatha Christie myself. I love a good mystery."

Darren said, "Renee is the librarian at the Bells public library."

"Oh, I'm envious," Michael said. "As a kid, I used to imagine owning a bookstore or working in a library or a university. Anywhere that I would be surrounded by books."

"How'd you end up in finance?" she asked, slowly sipping her coffee and sliding a cup to Michael across the kitchen island.

He shrugged. "It seemed like the right thing to do, I guess. My dad was a lawyer, and my mom was the CEO of an architecture and design firm, so the business world was just kind of expected. Plus, it seemed a lot more financially secure."

Michael unbuttoned his suit jacket as he sat down on a stool at the island, and suddenly, he looked down at himself and felt all wrong. Why was he still wearing a suit? Hadn't he just quit his job? Here he was visiting an old friend and still dressing all stiff and professional. It was laughable, really.

He shook his head and tried to shift his focus. "So, Darren, are you still working in Jackson?"

He nodded. "Yes, with the same accounting firm. It's been almost nine years there. That company has been really good to me."

"You don't mind the drive?"

"It's really not that far, and we can't imagine living anywhere but Bells."

"It is a really cute town. Oh, that reminds me." He grabbed the box from the bakery. "I stopped at the bakery downtown, too. The woman there knew you guys and said you would want snickerdoodle cookies and coconut cream pie?"

Renee lit up with a big smile as she took the box from him. "Oh, Emily? She's one of my closest friends. She's right about our favorite desserts. We go to Sweet Treats at least once a week."

"There are some cookies in there for the kids, too."

Renee pulled out a small pale blue box and asked, "Who's the chocolate cream pie for?"

Michael sat up straighter. "What?"

"There's a chocolate cream pie in here. Is that for you?"

He leaned across the counter to look at the pie, and it looked delicious. It was a smile pie, probably only about four inches wide, but it looked so good. She had slipped a pie in there? Just because he had said he liked them? What kind of person did that?

"I didn't know she put that in there."

"You mean you didn't order it?"

Michael shook his head. "No. I mean, she asked me what my favorite dessert was, and I told her, but I was kind of giving her a hard time. She must have put it in there as a joke."

Darren smiled. "No, that's just Emily. She's really good at running that bakery, and she knows exactly what everyone wants."

Michael smiled at Darren's comment, but he was really picturing Emily's smile when she had said he thought bakeries were conning people. He had practically insulted her, and yet, she responded with humor. It had been a long time since Michael had been around people like that. In fact, Darren had always been one of those people in his life. Darren was always full of joy and fun. With every passing second, Michael was becoming more and more glad that he had decided to make the trip to Tennessee after all. With the kids playing in the snow outside, the smell of cookies under his nose, and the smiles of Darren and Renee, Michael felt more at home than he had in a long time.

"So," Darren said, "what finally made you come down here after all? You seemed like you'd be pretty busy."

Michael let out a wry laugh. "Yeah, my plans didn't exactly work out the way I thought."

"Oh no," Renee said. "What happened?"

"Did you not get that promotion you mentioned?" Darren asked.

"Not only did I not get it, but I quit my job."

Simultaneously, both Darren and Renee said, "What?"

Michael shrugged and sipped his coffee. "I realized that I was working my butt off, and no one there really cared. I just suddenly wanted out." He rubbed the back of his neck. "I don't know, maybe it was kind of rash, but

I just had to walk away, you know? And since I don't have a job to work late hours for or a depressing office Christmas party to attend, I figured I'd might as well come here and relax."

"Sounds like you need it," Darren said. "So are you going to start applying in the new year?"

Michael sighed. That was the question, wasn't it? "I don't know. That was my plan, but the more that time passes since I quit, the more I'm starting to wonder if I even want another job in finance. I mean, am I really going to find anything different somewhere else? Aren't these firms all the same?"

"Not necessarily," Darren said. "I'm really happy with my company."

"True, but I guess I just don't love this world anymore. It's lost its shine."

Darren laughed. "Man, I don't think you ever loved that world. I always thought it seemed like a bad fit. I mean, you were good at it, don't get me wrong, but it never seemed like it made you happy."

"I was raised to view a career as work, I guess." Michael slumped in his chair. "Never as something to be enjoyed."

Renee leaned across the counter and smiled. There was something about her that put Michael at ease. She had a peacefulness to her. It made sense that she was a librarian. "What would your dream job be? Don't necessarily be realistic about it."

He sat up a little, but he struggled to come up with something. As a kid, he had used to picture himself working in a bookstore or a library or something and handing out books to kids. He could remember himself setting up little bookshelves and trying to sell books to his stuffed animals, but sometimes he gave the books away to the stuffed animals because he got so excited about them. It was one of those cute childhood fantasies. He never thought it could be real.

"I'm not sure, honestly. I briefly considered being an author or a journalist or something, but I didn't really like the idea of writing all of the time. I'd rather read."

"Maybe you could do book editing?" she said. "Or work for a publisher."

"Yeah, maybe. I don't know. I think I just need a break for Christmas. I need to take it easy for a while, eat some cookies, decorate a tree, stuff like that. Maybe I'll have a clearer head after the holidays."

Darren snagged the box of snickerdoodle cookies. "Fine, but you're not getting any of these."

Michael laughed and glanced down at the chocolate cream pie still sitting in its box in front of him and smiled. He really didn't want any of Darren's cookies anyway. Emily had already given him exactly what he wanted.

7

Emily

Hoping to beat the lunch rush, Emily made a quick run down the street to Stella's. She had accidentally skipped breakfast because she was so busy trying new drink recipes, and now that she hadn't eaten and had had too many sample sips of flavored coffee, she was feeling jittery and hungry. Stella's had the best cheeseburgers, and she could practically taste one.

She shrugged a jacket on as she walked out the door and walked a little too fast down the street, trying to be aware of ice on the sidewalk. She was already pushing it to get to Stella's before it became an absolute madhouse, and unfortunately for her, lunch was also a popular time for people to come into the bakery, so she had to make it back in time. She could even eat behind the counter if she had to.

She rounded the corner and, before she realized it, hit a patch of slick ice with her foot and slipped. She reached out to grab a lamp post or window sill for stability, but she missed and instead grabbed the coat of the man standing near her. She practically dragged him down with her until he realized what was happening and slipped an arm under hers to keep her from falling.

"Are you okay?" he asked once she had her feet back under her.

"Yeah, I'm fine, I—" she stopped short when she looked up at his sandy brown hair and sparkling blue eyes. "Chocolate cream pie."

"Excuse me?" he said.

"Oh, uh, you're the guy that ordered the chocolate cream pie."

"Actually I didn't order it. You just gave it to me. Thanks, by the way."

"Right," she said, but then she realized that she was still clutching his jacket, and he was still holding her up, so she scrambled to get her feet under her as gracefully as possible, only slipping once in the process. Standing this close to him, she could smell his cologne, something akin to sandalwood or a roaring fire.

"Are you sure you're okay?"

She took a step back, but he kept a hand on her elbow. "Yeah. That'll teach me for not putting on boots before going out here in a rush."

He laughed, and she found that she liked the way he laughed. It was gentle and sounded kind. "Where are you off to in such a hurry? I think I'd be safer if I went the opposite way."

"I was just trying to get some lunch before it gets too busy."

"Oh yeah? I was actually just out looking for something to eat. What's good around here?"

"Well, I was headed to Stella's. It's a diner just a couple of blocks down. Really good cheeseburgers, if you're into that kind of thing."

"Mind if I follow you there? I love a good cheeseburger. Plus, you're clearly a hazard to those around you, so I think I should keep an eye on you."

"It wasn't that bad of a fall," she said.

He smirked. "You nearly took us both out."

"Okay, fine," she said, and she noticed when he let go of her elbow. She'd liked the way it felt to be held by him regardless of the embarrassing circumstances.

They started walking in the direction of Stella's, and having exhausted the falling bit and the cheeseburgers, they both seemed to struggle to come up with a conversation starter.

Finally, Emily said, "So, were Darren and Renee happy with the desserts?"

"Very. How do you do that?"

"What?"

"Keep track of what everyone in town likes."

She laughed. "It isn't that hard. It's a really small town."

"Still."

"It's what I love," she said with a shrug. "I've worked in that bakery since I was a teenager. Honestly, since I was a little kid. I love it. I love getting to know what people like and what makes them happy. It's fun creating something people enjoy."

"That does sound nice."

Emily noticed his clothing. Another suit, but this time, without a tie. "So, what do you do? For a job, I mean."

Michael laughed. "I'm between jobs right now."

"Uh oh, did you get fired?"

"Why would you assume that?"

"That's what people who have been fired say."

"Or people who quit their jobs."

"Is that what you did?"

He smiled. "You're very invested in a total stranger's job."

"You're not a total stranger. You're here visiting Darren and Renee Moore. Your favorite dessert is chocolate cream pie. You hate holiday-themed coffee. You wear suits every day."

"You don't know that I wear suits every day."

"Every day that I've seen you."

He chuckled. "That's not very many days."

She looked away, focusing on her feet. She hadn't flirted with a guy like this in a while. Not since Noah. It felt kind of nice to walk down the street with an attractive man and be this flirtatious and silly. That had always been the problem with Noah: he was way too serious about all the wrong things and not serious about what had really mattered.

The problem was that Noah had been the same kind of guy as this man. Always wearing suits, always serious, but still charming when he wanted to be. Emily was starting to worry that maybe she had a type.

"Penny for your thoughts?" he said, and she realized she'd been quiet for some time.

"They'll cost you more than a penny."

He smiled. Gosh, he looked so good when he smiled. "How about coffee?"

She noticed they had made it to Stella's, and he opened the door for her, so she stepped in. "How about you stop by the bakery later? I have to get back pretty quickly in case it gets busy, but it slows down around 2."

He smiled. "I'll be there. I'm Michael, by the way."

"Emily."

"See you later, Emily."

She watched—for longer than she'd like to admit—as he walked up to the counter to order. What finally snapped her daze was Bella flagging her down from a table by the window.

"Hey," Emily said as she sat across from Bella.

"So are you going to join me for lunch and tell me about that super hot guy you were just talking to?"

"I can't stay. I'm just picking up a to-go order. And there's nothing to say about him."

"Who is he?"

"Some guy from out of town. He's visiting Darren and Renee. Old friend, I guess."

"Did I just hear him say that he'll see you later?"

"He asked me out for coffee. I told him to come to the bakery later."

"Why didn't you just say yes?"

"I don't have time. I barely had time to come here to get food. I'm too busy getting ready for Deck the Shops."

"Emily, it's been two years since you and Noah broke up. You have to move on at some point."

"Two years isn't that long. We were engaged."

"But your life can't be on pause forever. That guy—"

"Michael."

"He's good looking. He seems nice."

"He caught me when I totally wiped out on the street and grabbed his coat on the way down, so that was pretty embarrassing."

"That's not that big of a deal. What's the problem?"

"Uh, he doesn't live here? He thinks bakeries are corrupt?"

"What?"

"Long story."

"What harm can a date do?"

"Look, he's coming to the bakery later. We'll see what happens. But I'm not letting myself get distracted from Deck the Shops. I have to win."

"Sweet Treats wins every year. I don't think you have to worry."

"All the more reason that I need to win. I have to prove to my grandparents that I have good ideas for the bakery. They'll never trust me with the bakery until I can convince them that I know what I'm doing."

"Emily," the cashier called out and held up a paper bag.

"I've got to go," Emily said as she stood. "Talk to you later?"

"You have to tell me what happens with that guy!" Bella called out as Emily walked away.

"I will," she said, but she knew there probably wouldn't be much to tell. It couldn't go anywhere with this guy. He wasn't going to stay in Bells just like Noah wouldn't stay in Bells. She knew where those relationships went.

But Deck the Shops—that was her ticket to success and proving herself. She knew she had to make it work.

8

Michael

Michael walked Main Street downtown and admired all of the Christmas decor. Not only had each business decorated its windows and doors with festive decorations but it seemed the town itself had caught the spirit. The light posts and street signs all had garland or lights wrapped around them, there were poinsettias everywhere, and it seemed that Santas ringing bells for donations were inescapable. Michael thought it was maybe a bit overdone, but he liked that Bells fully committed to the holiday season. It made everything just seem nice the way that only Christmas could.

Still, the Christmas cheer couldn't distract him from his thoughts. The fact of the matter was that Michael was jobless, and once the Christmas season was over and he flew back to Chicago, he'd have to face that. He'd told Darren and Renee that he wasn't sure he still wanted to work in finance, but that felt absolutely ridiculous and wildly unrealistic. He had an MBA and had always worked in finance, so why would he do something else? It would be like starting over. Maybe he was being pessimistic, but he just couldn't stand the thought of ending up at another place like the company he'd just left.

In an attempt to get his life back on course, he was actually headed to Sweet Treats, laptop bag over his shoulder, to get some coffee and work on his resume and maybe start poking around some job listings. Maybe something would spark his interest and remind him why he'd gone into finance in the first place. He certainly couldn't remember. If nothing else, maybe he'd see Emily again. Something about her made him smile just to think about her.

But when he got close to the bakery, he stopped abruptly when he noticed a "For Sale" sign in the window of Something Worth Reading. He didn't know why, but he found his feet carrying him across the street to the bookstore instead of the bakery. When he pushed the door open, the owner looked up at him and smiled.

"So, did the boys like the books?" she asked.

Michael nodded. "They did. Thanks for the help. I'm Michael, by the way."

She jutted out a hand for a handshake. "Naomi."

He pointed to the window. "I just saw the sign. You're selling the bookstore?"

She let out a heavy sigh as she nodded. "I think it's time. I started this place nearly forty years ago, you know."

"Wow, that's impressive."

"I thought Bells needed a bookstore. I've run it ever since."

"You never considered selling before?"

"No, this is my life's work. I've had plenty of offers over the years, but they always came from big developers who wanted to knock it down or big chain bookstores who wanted to take out all the charm. I could never trust anyone else with it. I'm so proud of it."

"Then why sell now?"

Naomi pointed to some armchairs in the corner, and they both sat down. "Age catches up to you. You'll find that out one day, Michael. I'm just getting older, and my daughters live in Florida, so I'm going to move to be closer to them. I want to be near them and my grandkids. Plus, I'm really looking forward to the warm weather," she said with a laugh.

"That makes sense." But honestly, it didn't totally make sense to Michael. He understood wanting to be closer to family, though it was never something he particularly wanted. And he understood wanting to slow down even though he was at a point in his career when he was supposed to be speeding up. But he struggled to understand how Naomi could let go of this after all this time. She was living the dream, and she was ready to walk away?

Naomi furrowed her eyebrows. "You all right, son? You seem a little down."

Michael shook his head a little, bringing him back to focus. "Yes, sorry, I got a little lost in my thoughts."

She smiled. "Well, can I help you find something? I'm still a bookseller for now, you know."

"No, I'm okay, thanks."

Naomi walked back over to the shelf she had been stocking when he had entered, and Michael found himself staring blankly at his hands in his lap. He couldn't really figure out why it bothered him so much that a woman he had just met was selling a bookstore in a town he'd only just visited. Maybe it was some kind of childhood nostalgia, but Something Worth Reading reminded him of going to bookstores as a kid and experiencing the magic of good storytelling. Indie bookstores like this were becoming more and more rare, and while he'd been known to buy a book at a chain store or online, it never held the same magic. He guessed that he feared the same thing that had prevented Naomi from selling all these years: that someone would ruin it or remove it. It happened all too often.

Michael was aware of a thought bouncing around his brain, though he hadn't yet allowed himself to focus on it. This was exactly what he pictured when Renee asked him what his dream job would be. He hadn't allowed himself to admit it to her out loud, but it was the first thought that had entered his brain. As a child, owning a bookstore had seemed like the obvious choice. As an adult, it seemed impractical, a pipe dream based on nostalgia and warm, fuzzy feelings, not sound business sense or career-building. But Naomi had done it for forty years. She had lived the dream and been successful. Maybe it wasn't such a fantasy after all.

He pushed himself up from the chair and walked quickly over to Naomi before his parents' voices ringing in his ear could talk him out of the rash decision he was making. "What if I were interested in buying the bookstore?" he said.

Naomi turned to look him up and down, then smiled and rested her hands on her hips. "So what if you were?"

He let out a small sigh. "I'm interested in buying the bookstore. What is your list price?"

"Now hold on, I haven't said I was interested in selling to you."

"But the sign—"

"I'm selling, but I'm determined to find the right person. I absolutely refuse to sell to a developer or a chain bookstore. Are you either of those?"

"No."

"Good start. Are you a Scrooge?"

"Excuse me?"

Naomi walked down the aisles, stocking books as she went even though it seemed as if her path was aimless. Michael followed closely behind. "Are you a Scrooge? A grinch. The kind of uptight guy who picks on the little guy and hoards money."

"Uh, no."

"Well, that's good. But I still don't know anything about you. How am I supposed to hand off my business to a total stranger?"

Michael slipped his laptop bag onto his shoulder, straightened his posture, and smiled. "I'm Michael Anderson. I'm from Chicago. I went to Northwestern University where I earned a bachelor's and an MBA, both in finance. I recently quit Rothstein Investments, a large firm that dealt with moderately sized businesses and mergers."

Naomi squinted. "Why did you quit?"

"I realized that they didn't want someone who was good at their job but rather someone who would flatter the boss, and that just isn't me."

She shrugged and started stocking shelves again. "Well, I do like that."

"Look, to be honest with you, I didn't come to Bells looking for a job. I'm visiting my college roommate Darren Moore. He invited me to spend the holidays with his family, and that's all this trip was going to be, but the more I'm away from the finance world and Chicago, the more I'm thinking that I don't want to go back. I like it here, and maybe that's the real reason I was supposed to come to Bells. Maybe I needed to see that I needed a radical change in my life. I've always loved reading and books, and as a kid, I used to dream of running a bookstore. I just needed a push to make me realize that I should go after what I always wanted instead of working a job I hate for the rest of my life."

"Hmm," was all Naomi said.

Michael sighed. "I know I'm rambling, but you're looking at retirement after doing what you loved for forty years. That's what I want. I don't want to look back on my life and regret working my life away. I want to do something that matters that I enjoy. I have so many ideas for what I could do with a bookstore. I want to make them a reality."

Naomi studied him carefully, and the longer that she didn't say anything, the more Michael was second-guessing everything he was doing. He felt simultaneously like he had lost his mind and also that he was finally doing something he wanted to do instead of what he thought he was supposed to do.

Impulsively, Michael added, "I'll pay you market value," though he had no idea what that was on a store like this.

Finally, Naomi raised her index finger and said, "I'll tell you what. I'm not going to sell my business to someone I don't know and I can trust to treat it the way I would."

"Totally understandable."

"But I'm willing to give you a shot and hear you out."

"Fantastic. Should we have lunch or something so we can talk through my ideas?"

She shook her head and grabbed a flyer off of the wall. "Every year, we have a competition called 'Deck the Shops.' It's a friendly competition in town. Local businesses have little pop-up events to promote the store."

"What's the prize?"

"Bragging rights," she said as if it should have been obvious. "There's a cash prize, but it's nothing to get too excited about. I wasn't going to do it this year because it's a lot of work, and frankly, I'm tired. But it's a fun event, and I don't really want the store to miss out. So here's my offer. You take over Something Worth Reading's contest entry. I'll give you access to the bookstore, any resources I have, connections, everything you would need to create a pop-up event. Show me that you really believe in this and want to preserve the integrity of my store. If I like what you do, I'll sell you the bookstore."

"That's it?" he said, taking the flyer from her.

She nodded. "That's it. Now that the store is officially listed for sale, I know those big developers are going to come sniffing around. I don't want to sell to them. I want to sell to someone like me. Prove that you're someone like me."

She went back to stocking the shelves, and Michael skimmed the flyer. He had no idea how big this contest was or how involved it was. What would it really take to win? He started to wonder what he was really getting himself into.

He called out to her, "Do I have to win the contest?"

She turned around and flashed him a wry smile. "Good luck, Mr. Anderson."

9

Emily

After wiping down all of the tables from the mid-afternoon rush, Emily collapsed into the corner of the booth that ran the full wall length. She felt like she had been running all day. Most weekdays weren't that busy, but the stream of customers just hadn't really stopped, and she was exhausted. At least the bakery looked put together now that she had straightened all the tables, wiped everything down, and refilled the bakery case. She'd collected all of the napkin dispensers from the tables and set about refilling those. It seemed like that was the thing she refilled most often, which seemed silly considered the number of cookies the bakery sold per day.

She started stuffing napkins into the dispensers, and her mind drifted, but to what, she couldn't decide. She wasn't really thinking about anything in particular, but she thought about her ideas for Deck the Shops, her grandparents, her parents, and everything in between. As a kid, she'd always imagined that one day she would take over the bakery, but she had never really put much thought into what that would actually look like. She imagined a partnership between her and her grandparents. She imagined a husband, and she pictured having kids who would play in the bakery the same way she had. She'd thought Noah was the one when they dated.

He had checked all of the boxes, but he envisioned a life in the city. He'd moved to Philadelphia after they got engaged, assuming she would follow him there. He'd never understood her connections to Sweet Treats or even to Bells. He assumed that she'd change her life to suit his, and that was what had ended their engagement, long before she'd had a chance to buy a dress. She guessed that something had always felt wrong to her, which was why she'd turned down every offer from her grandmother or her girl friends to go dress shopping. She was glad, at least, that she didn't have an unworn dress in her closet, a ghost of Christmas never-happened haunting her at every turn. It had so totally never happened that there was now no proof that she'd ever been engaged.

The door chimed, and she barely glanced up, half expecting someone to be coming in just for the free wi-fi, but when she saw Michael, she couldn't help the smile that spread on her face, no matter how much she didn't want to be happy to see him.

When he spotted her, he waved and walked over to the booth next to her. "Are you sure you're not too busy right now? It seems like a madhouse."

"Ha, ha," Emily said, rolling her eyes. "Enjoy your cheeseburger?"

"Oh," Michael sighed dramatically, touching his stomach. "Delicious. Nobody makes a burger like a diner."

"That's what I always say."

Michael sat down on the booth at the table next to Emily's and set his bag on the table. "Do you have wi-fi here?"

She nodded. "For customers. Can I get you something?"

"Do you have coffee that isn't weirdly Christmasy?"

"Are you always so anti-Christmas cheer?"

"I'm not anti-Christmas cheer. I'm anti-weirdly flavored coffee, that's all."

"How about a mocha? That's normal."

He raised an eyebrow. "You have that?"

"Not officially, but I'm trying out some potential new menu items. You could be a taste tester."

"Only because I like mochas."

Emily smiled and headed off to get the coffee. A mocha was probably the best chance she had of convincing her grandparents to add a menu item. It was relatively normal and had wide appeal. She felt confident that she could sway them on that. Maybe if she got some positive feedback from people like Michael or others at Deck the Shops then they would see that it would be successful.

She poured the coffee into a wide rimmed cup and squirted some whipped cream on the top. She'd been practicing latte art on her own coffee at home, and she'd gotten decently good at it, but Michael didn't seem like the type to want latte art, so she skipped it for now. She knew she could impress some people with that skill at the pop-up event.

She brought the mocha to Michael on a plate trimmed with Christmas trees, and he rolled his eyes when he saw it. "Seriously?"

"Just because you're a Christmas grump doesn't mean the rest of us are."

He sat back in the booth and put an arm across the back. "A Christmas grump?"

"Yes. You're grumpy about Christmas."

"I am not."

"Then why are you grumpy?"

He sighed. "I'm trying to figure out my next move career wise. I quit my job because I wasn't happy with the firm and I knew that I wouldn't have any upward mobility if I stayed there, but I'm thinking that maybe I'm done with the finance world entirely."

"Finance?" Emily sat down next to him. "That's what you did before?"

He nodded. "In Chicago. I came here to see Darren, and, I don't know, maybe I just need to make a total change."

"What does that look like?"

"Do you know the bookstore across the street?"

"Something Worth Reading? Of course. Growing up, any time I didn't spend in the bakery I spent there."

"The woman who owns it—"

"Naomi."

"Yes, Naomi. She's selling."

Emily sat back. "Really? She's been thinking of selling for some time, but it kind of seemed like one of those things she'd never really do, you know?"

"She said she wants to move to Florida to be closer to her kids."

"That makes sense."

"Well, I was considering buying it."

"Really?" Emily thought for a moment. This was different than her past relationships. Here was a guy who was potentially choosing the small town life for himself, independent of her. But was it too good to be true? "And what, move from Chicago to Bells?"

"Yeah, maybe," he said, then took a sip of his coffee. "This is delicious."

"Thanks."

"No, seriously, mocha coffee is one of my favorites, and this might be the best one I've ever had. The whipped cream is a nice touch."

"Glad to hear it. I figured you would like it."

"Why?"

"Because you love chocolate cream pie. That's basically that in drink form."

"What are you, a bakery savant?"

Emily held her face totally serious and flat. "Yes. And I take it very seriously."

Michael laughed, and again, Emily found herself charmed by the sound of his laughter.

"So," Emily said, "You didn't really answer my question."

"Sure, I did."

She shook her head. "Not really. Why Bells?"

He shrugged. "Why not Bells, I guess? Darren and I have been best friends since we went to Northwestern together. I don't really have any friends like that in Chicago."

"What about family?"

"My parents both passed years ago."

"I'm sorry to hear that."

"It's all right. We weren't close."

"Wow."

"What?" he asked.

"My parents live in Florida, but we're still close. We talk all the time."

"Just didn't work out that way for me, I guess," Michael said, but Emily still found that odd. He seemed so cavalier about his lack of relationship with his parents. He didn't even really seem phased that they were gone. Even though Emily had probably spent more time with her grandparents than her parents growing up, she never doubted her relationship with her parents. She knew that they cared, and she valued them highly in her life.

"Well, enough of my childhood drama," Michael said, a chuckle punctuating his words. "So you said you're testing new menu items?"

"Trying to," Emily said with a sigh. "My grandparents don't really want to change anything."

"Is the bakery not yours?"

She shook her head. "My grandparents own it. I'm the manager. I have so many ideas for how to improve the business, but they're pretty traditional and don't really see the point in changing anything. I just have to find a way to show them that my ideas will benefit the bakery overall."

Michael laughed. "Somehow I think you'll find a way. You don't seem like the type to give up easily."

"Definitely not. So you come to visit your college roommate and decide on a whim to move to his hometown? Doesn't seem to match your serious, finance-bro image."

Michael sat back a little and laughed. "Finance-bro image? What on earth does that mean?"

She gestured up and down his body, indicating his trademark suit. "Isn't it obvious?"

"You really think you've got me figured out, don't you?"

The problem was that she was pretty sure she did. Bells was the kind of place that made it easy to fall in love with it and want to stay forever, especially at Christmas. Emily was pretty sure you'd have to be heartless not to get swept up in the town's charm. But what happened when the Christmas lights came down, when the snow turned to slush, and real life took over again? Would Michael still want to be here, or would he feel trapped by Bells? Emily was too afraid to risk her heart again on someone who might not be in it for the long haul.

She didn't have time to entertain ideas of dating anyone, even if it was someone like Michael. Sweet Treats had won Deck the Shops more than any other business in town. She *had* to win if she was going to have even a chance of convincing her grandparents to take a chance on her ideas.

And no one was going to distract her from winning first place, and that included handsome, charming strangers from Chicago.

10

Michael

"What on earth were you thinking?" Darren asked between fits of laughter, nearly knocking himself off the kitchen stool he was sitting on. He'd been surprised when Michael told him about his interest in buying Something Worth Reading, but Michael hadn't expected this reaction.

"Is it so weird that I would buy a bookstore?" Michael asked.

"No, that's the most normal part of what you've said. But how on earth are you going to win Deck the Shops?"

"I have no idea. I was hoping you would know. I don't know anything about this competition."

Darren laughed again. "It's not exactly much of a competition. The same business wins almost every year."

"Then what do I do to stand out? Bookstores are pretty straightforward. I'm not exactly sure what creative thing I can do to win."

"Well, did Naomi say you have to win?"

Michael huffed. "She refused to say. I'm assuming that means yes."

Darren drummed his thumb on the edge of the island countertop. "Well, I've known Naomi since I was a little kid, and if there's one thing I know about her, it's that she won't be impressed by something flashy. She'll want something meaningful, something with heart."

"Will heart and meaning win the contest?"

"I guess we'll find out." Darren walked into the kitchen to grab a snickerdoodle cookie. "By the way," he said around a mouthful of cookie, "while you're busy trying to buy a bookstore, see if you can pick up more cookies."

Michael laughed. "Why don't you pick them up?"

"I don't work right across the street from Sweet Treats, and for the next couple of weeks, you do."

"Fine, I'll get some the next time I'm there."

Darren raised an eyebrow and leaned over the counter. "Next time? Exactly how many times have you frequented this bakery?"

"Just a few times." Michael hadn't intended to say more, but Darren's raised eyebrow said that he wasn't done just yet. "What?"

"I suppose the pretty baker has nothing to do with your sudden need for desserts, does she?"

"What are you trying to insinuate?"

"Look, I don't think it's such a bad thing. Have you dated anyone since Maggie?"

"What difference does that make?"

"I know that it was tough on you when she called it quits. I'm just saying that it's not such a terrible thing to ask a girl on a date. Especially Emily—she's so sweet."

Michael snorted. "Did you really just call a baker 'sweet'?"

"Don't try to change the subject."

"I just met the girl. I can't just ask her out. We don't know anything about each other."

"Isn't that what dates are for?"

"Besides, I don't even know if I'm staying here."

Darren laughed loudly. "What are you doing trying to buy a bookstore here, then?"

"I'm not sure I even know," Michael said, rubbing the sides of his face. "Am I totally insane?"

"I've always thought so."

Michael smiled but said, "I'm serious, Darren. I just quit my job, and for what? Because my pride got hurt? Because I thought that company owed me something? And then I come here just to see you, and now I'm entering some small town contest to convince some stubborn old woman to sell me her bookstore. Is that my next move? I'm going to run a bookstore? I have an MBA in finance, for goodness sake."

"You have an MBA in finance because your parents insisted on the safe and predictable corporate world. You never loved it. I certainly heard you complain enough about it when we lived together."

"Yeah, but that's the point, isn't? It is safe and predictable. I'm just throwing out a perfectly good career, and why?"

"To chase your dreams."

Michael rolled his eyes. "Ugh, that sounds like a cheesy rom-com movie."

"Following your dreams isn't a bad thing, you know. What's wrong with doing something with your life that makes you happy?"

"If one of my coworkers in Chicago had told me they were quitting their job to buy a bookstore in the middle of nowhere on a whim, I would have called them crazy."

"Well, you're not in Chicago, are you? This is Bells, and around here, family and happiness matter a whole lot more than status or billable hours."

Michael hesitated a moment, unsure what to say to that. He used to believe that places like Bells weren't real, that they only existed in fictional idyllic towns in Hallmark movies and only at Christmas. Darren had tried to tell him for years to visit Bells, but he'd always considered himself a city person. But now, sitting in his best friend's kitchen listening to Darren's boys playing in the snow outside and eating cookies and picturing Emily's pretty smile—well, it was hard to think of going back to Chicago now. It'd been more than a year since Maggie had broken up with him because she claimed he worked too many hours, and at the time, he'd thought she was wrong, but was she? That job had consumed his entire life. He didn't have friends in Chicago. There was nothing tying him to that place except his own stubbornness and the weight of his parents' expectations, but none of that seemed to matter anymore.

"Serious question, Darren," Michael said. "Are you happy in Bells? No regrets?"

"No regrets," Darren said immediately and so confidently that it surprised Michael even though that had been the answer he had expected—or rather, wanted—to hear. "Could I be making more money elsewhere? Sure, probably. But I wouldn't be happier. I can provide for my family, and I have time and energy to spend with my boys and my wife. I wouldn't want it any other way. I always knew that I wanted to come back here to Bells after college because I grew up here. I think it's hard for you to see it since you didn't grow up here, but Bells is a great place to be."

Michael looked around Darren's house. It was the picture-perfect family home. It was nice, and Renee had clearly put a lot of effort into the decor, but the boys' Hot Wheels cars were strewn across the living room rug, and the fridge was covered with mismatched Christmas magnets holding crayon drawings. Michael's home growing up probably cost two or three times as much as this house, and yet, he thought he had never seen a more perfect home.

Michael rubbed the side of his neck and sighed. "I guess I'm entering Deck the Shops, then."

Darren slapped him on the back. "Attaboy. You can pick up an entry form at the town hall building downtown. It's just past the bookstore."

"Great."

Darren grabbed two more cookies. "And don't forget to stop by the bakery and get more cookies."

Michael crossed his arms. "I'm starting to think you're only letting me stay in your guest room as long as I keep buying you cookies."

"You're only just now starting to think that? I thought you were smarter than that, man."

Michael laughed, but he reached for his coat, on a mission to buy yet another round of desserts. If he didn't win Deck the Shops and therefore the ability to purchase Something Worth Reading, it was going to be hard to justify—even to himself—staying in Bells long term. And when he thought of Emily's smile and the sparkle in her eyes, well—he wanted to be able to justify staying in Bells.

11

Emily

It was after hours, and Main Street in downtown Bells was quiet except for people headed to and from late night dinner reservations. Most shops closed around 6 PM or so, leaving just the restaurants and the only bar in town open at night, and even those didn't stay open very late compared to the hours in a bigger city.

Sweet Treats had been slow for the last hour it was open, so Emily had had a chance to clean up and sweep everything and refill all of the napkin dispensers. All that was left was to shut down all of the display cases to preserve the pastries and do final inventory reports for the night.

To Emily's surprise, her grandparents walked in through the main door, using their key to enter. They didn't typically come in after hours anymore as Emily always took the closing shift. She knew they preferred the mornings and that closing up the bakery late at night was just too tiring for them. Besides, she didn't mind. She actually kind of liked the quiet of the closing shift. She always found it stressful to try to bake in the mornings, feeling like she was racing the clock to finish before it was time to open, but at night, there was no deadline. She lived upstairs, so she had no commute to worry about. She could take as long as she wanted baking whatever was running low so that it would be ready in the morning.

"Hi, honey," her grandmother said, brushing some little snowflakes off of her shoulder.

"Hi," Emily said. "I wasn't expecting to see you."

"Your grandfather forgot his keys in the office," she said as Grandpa shuffled past her to the office. "We walked to dinner at the steakhouse, and he didn't realize he didn't have them until we couldn't get into our car." She chuckled, smiling sweetly at the forgetfulness of her husband of fifty-five years. "You're not working too late again, are you?"

Emily smiled. "No, I'm done. I'm just finishing inventory. Hey, what would you think about Sweet Treats staying open later a couple of nights a week?"

"Whatever for?"

"The after-dinner crowd. It wouldn't really matter early in the week, but I'm thinking Friday and Saturday nights, if we stayed open until 7 or 8, we could probably make some late night dessert sales."

Grandpa came out of the office. "What about dessert sales?"

Emily resisted the urge to let out a frustrated sigh. She had hoped she could sell Grandma on the idea before he shot it down. "I was just saying that if we stayed open later just on Fridays and Saturdays, we might be able to capitalize on people leaving dinner who might want, you know, a sweet treat." After an awkward silence, she added, "See what I did there?"

"There's no reason to stay open later," Grandpa said. "We've never needed to."

"I'm not saying we need to, but we could. You both wouldn't have to do anything. I would take the extra hours."

"It's just unnecessary. If people are out having dinner at a restaurant, then they'll order dessert at the restaurant if they want it."

"Sure, but would you order a mediocre dessert at a restaurant if you knew the local bakery was open late?"

Grandpa set his keys down on the counter in a huff. "I just don't see the point. There's no reason to change our hours."

"But if we just tried it—"

"Why are you trying to change everything lately?" he said suddenly and more loudly than Emily was expecting. "It's starting to feel like nothing that your grandmother and I have built here is good enough for you. You've been trying to change the menu, the hours, everything. We're not changing the hours, and that's that. Come on, Eleanor," he said, snatching his keys again.

"I'll be right there, dear," she said. Once he had stepped out, she said to Emily, "He'll calm down."

"I'm not trying to change everything you both did here."

"I know that, honey, and he does, too."

Emily let herself drop onto a stool. "I just want to feel like I'm contributing here."

"Oh, you are," she said sweetly.

"I mean more than just keeping the place running. I want to follow in your footsteps and really do something meaningful here, but he doesn't even want to hear any of my ideas."

"He put so much into this place. He's just protective of it. And you. You're always going to be his little girl."

"I'm not a little girl anymore."

She touched the side of Emily's cheek gently. "Just give it time." She glanced back at her husband waiting outside. "We should get home before the snow gets worse, but I'm very excited to see what you do with the Deck the Shops event."

Emily forced a smile, and Grandma went out the door with her husband who locked it behind her. Emily slid the inventory reports across the counter to where she was sitting and tried to focus, but her eyes kept blurring as she stared at the page.

When she'd thought of the idea of running the event for Deck the Shops, she had been really optimistic that it would be her chance to prove herself to her grandfather. She'd thought that her ideas were just not real to him, but if he saw tangible proof of what she could do, then he'd understand. Now, she was feeling more and more nervous for the event by the day. It was a big risk that he would see everything and hate it even more than he already did. She was starting to think it was going to be impossible to change his mind.

As a kid, Emily had thought her grandparents were superheroes. They had seemed able to do it all: run the bakery, help her mother raise her, volunteer at their church, and stay dedicated to their marriage. Emily could only dream of having a life that looked like theirs one day.

But the realities of adulthood simultaneously made Emily respect them more and also recognize just how hard that balancing act must have been. Lately, she'd been neglecting her usual volunteer work, found it hard to make time for friends, hadn't dated since Noah, and generally just wasn't doing so hot in her personal life. The one thing she felt she was good at was running Sweet Treats. It was where she always knew she belonged. As a child, she'd always said that one day she'd run Sweet Treats, and she had always been met with patronizing smiles from adults who had assumed it was a childish thing that would pass. As a teenager looking down the barrel at college and adulthood, the only thing she could conceive of herself doing for the rest of her life was this bakery. It was the only thing that felt easy, that felt right.

She sighed and filled out the final numbers on the inventory list and filed it in the office. No matter how scary it would be, Deck the Shops really was her only chance. Sweet Treats was everything to her, and she had to prove, to her grandparents and herself, that not only was she capable of running this business for the next few decades but that she could make it thrive. She had to prove that she had inherited that magic touch from them. Proving that to the town wouldn't be hard, and she was pretty sure her grandmother wasn't a hard sell either. Proving it to her grandfather was going to be incredibly difficult. Proving it to herself? That was the part Emily was starting to doubt, and yet, it was becoming more and more important to her.

12

Michael

The wind was picking up, and Michael tugged at the collar of his coat. It still didn't compare to the harsh, icy winds of Chicago, but cold wind was cold wind, and he shivered against the chill. He saw the flames of some space heaters in the square, so he shuffled in their direction.

He hadn't been sure he would attend Bells's annual tree lighting, but it was where they did the official sign-ups for Deck the Shops, so he was somewhat obligated to attend. He wasn't sure what he had pictured when he pictured the tree lighting in a small town, but this was certainly bigger than anything he'd thought it would be. The tree downtown was pretty large, and there seemed to be some kind of vendor craft market going on also. It was cute. Everything about Bells was still so foreign and kind of strange to him, but he couldn't say he didn't enjoy the town. Everyone here seemed really happy and friendly, and he liked how committed they were to Christmas. Every street sign and light post was wrapped with red and white ribbon, all of the business had wreaths and some kind of Christmas decoration, and even the lights stretching across the street between the buildings downtown were red, white, and green. It was so beautiful.

He spotted a stand that was serving hot chocolate, so he headed in that direction, looking forward to a hot drink to temper this cold weather. As he approached, he noticed Emily in line and smiled to himself. An even better reason to get hot chocolate.

"Well, funny running into you here."

"Not really," Emily said with a wry smile. Michael's smile grew wider when her eyes met his. He'd always had a thing for blue eyes. "It's a pretty small town."

"Ha-ha," Michael said dryly. "Is the whole town at this thing? I swear I haven't seen this many people the entire time I've been here."

"Oh, absolutely. The annual tree lighting is a can't-miss event. You can't live in Bells and not make an appearance at the tree lighting."

"I'm still getting used to that, I guess." Michael turned to the elderly woman at the hot cocoa tent. "Two, please," he said and handed her a five dollar bill.

"So, what is Chicago like?" Emily said as they stepped aside to wait for their drinks. "I've never been there."

"Really? I've never lived anywhere else."

"Same."

Michael shoved his hands in his pockets. The wind didn't bite the same way here as it did in Chicago, but it was still pretty chilly tonight, and he had forgotten to bring gloves with him. He was looking forward to holding a hot beverage. "I never used to be able to picture myself anywhere but Chicago. I love all the food and the city vibe, but when I think about it, I never spent any time anywhere that wasn't a city."

"Really? I've been to Nashville and Raleigh, but everywhere else I've visited has very much a small town vibe."

Michael laughed. "That's so hard for me to picture, but these last few days in Bells have me rethinking that."

Emily smiled wide. "We're getting to you, huh?"

"You're definitely getting to me," Michael said, his eyes locked on Emily's. He was pretty sure that he had been feeling sparks between him and Emily, but it was definitely feeling more and more like it was something beyond just friendly flirtation. He couldn't help but smile every time he was around her, every time she looked at him.

Just when he was considering making a move for her hand, the young boy pouring the hot chocolate held out two cups to them.

"Thanks," he and Emily said simultaneously.

"The toppings bar is right there," the boy said, pointing at a table.

Michael looked at the table and was shocked to see how many toppings were being offered for a simple cup of hot cocoa. He was fully intending to pass it by when Emily stopped and started scooping marshmallows.

"You've got to be kidding," he said.

"No, you've got to be kidding," she said, still scooping marshmallows. Michael wondered how there was still space in her cup for more. "You're not going to get any toppings?"

"Why would I?"

"Uh, because it's hot chocolate at a Christmas tree lighting. Toppings are mandatory." She dropped a peppermint stick in her cup and started squirting whipped cream from a can on top.

Michael laughed. "You're insane. How can you even taste the cocoa at this point?"

She held the can out toward him. "At least put in some whipped cream. It would be a crime not to."

He rolled his eyes, but the way she raised her eyebrows and wiggled the can made him laugh, and he couldn't resist indulging her. "Fine, just a little bit." When she squirted whipped cream for several seconds, he said, "Oh my gosh, you're out of control."

She laughed, set the can down, and they started wandering through downtown, browsing at some of the stands selling crafts and Christmas snacks. "So, what made you such a Grinch?"

"I am not a Grinch!"

"Anyone who doesn't want marshmallows and whipped cream in their hot cocoa at Christmastime is definitely a Grinch."

"That's a really bizarre standard for Grinchiness."

"It's perfectly logical," she said, then stopped suddenly and faced him. "Or maybe you're a Scrooge."

"I think that might be worse," Michael said with a chuckle.

"Eh," Emily said, weighing her hands back and forth, "it's really a toss-up." She didn't say anything for a few moments, then added, "Well?"

"I don't know. I guess Christmas just wasn't really a big deal for me as a kid."

"That seems contrary to childhood."

Michael laughed again and marveled at how easy it was for her to make him laugh. "Honestly, it kind of is. My parents were always so busy, especially around the holidays, so Christmas wasn't really a priority."

"Did you not celebrate at all?"

Michael hesitated in front of a stall selling handmade ornaments and fidgeted with a few of them. They were beautiful. "No, we celebrated, but Christmas was very formal, very, I don't know, professional, I guess. My parents always hired a company to decorate our house, and they were always busy with office Christmas parties or last-minute end-of-the-year deals to broker. We never did stuff like this."

"Presents on Christmas morning? Unwrapping? A special Christmas breakfast?"

"I usually opened the presents they got for me by myself. They usually slept in because they were tired from whatever Christmas Eve party they had attended or hosted. And breakfast, well, I knew how to heat up a toaster strudel."

Emily held a blue ornament with white hand-painted snowflakes in her hand, staring at the glittering snow on it. "That's kind of sad."

"Not really. Have you ever had a cinnamon roll flavored toaster strudel? They're pretty good."

She smirked a little. "Not the toaster strudel. I can't picture Christmas day without my parents and grandparents and homemade cinnamon rolls and a tree with homemade ornaments—hang on. I've got an idea."

"What?"

"Come with me."

Emily grabbed Michael's hand and led him through the maze of stalls, and in between appreciating the fact that he was holding her hand and enjoying the smell of her perfume wafting from her as she walked, he wondered how she didn't get totally lost in this mess of stalls that all looked the same. When she stopped suddenly, Michael nearly spilled his hot chocolate on his hand.

"Here we are," Emily said, gesturing at the stall in front of them. It seemed to be hosted by some kind of craft store and had a sign that read "Ornament Making."

Michael raised an eyebrow. "Is this a make-your-own-ornament booth?"

"Indeed it is."

"I swear, this town feels less like a real place and more like something out of a cheesy movie every day."

She put her hands on her hips. "If you're going to spend Christmas with Renee and Darren, you're going to need to be prepared. They decorate their tree every year with homemade ornaments and ornaments that have been passed down in the family. I'm assuming you don't have either of those, so it's time you make one."

Michael glanced at the booth and took note of the current customers. "Everyone here is under the age of twelve."

"Well, it's not my fault that you're behind. Now, come on."

Again, she took his hand and led him to the back of the stall where there were some empty seats. She sat down at the corner which left the seat next to a six-year-old available to him. He sighed, sat down, and immediately felt the eyes of this small child on him.

"Hey, Piper," Emily said to the woman running the booth, "we've got a newbie here."

"Well then, isn't that exciting?" Piper said. "Welcome to our booth. We sell craft supplies and year-round home decor over at Paint & Pine. Come see us if you're in need of any decorations."

Michael thought about the competition. He hadn't noticed very much in the way of decorations at Something Worth Reading, so he thought he might have to drop in and pick up some supplies.

"I'll definitely do that," he said.

"He's from Chicago," Emily said, "visiting the Moores, and he's got nothing to contribute to their Christmas tree."

Piper said, "Obviously we have to change that."

Piper set a round ornament in front of him and proceeded to explain to him all of the different art supplies available to him, but Michael struggled to keep up. How could there possibly be this many ways to decorate a simple glass ball ornament? All of the textile options seemed like a bad idea, and he felt confident that if he even touched the glitter he would never get it to wash out of his coat, so he decided painting was the best route. He looked to Emily for guidance, but she was already painting and looked very focused.

The little boy next to him tapped his shoulder and said, "How many ornaments have you made?"

"This would be the first."

"What?" the boy said, more loudly than he would have preferred. "I beat you. I made this many," he said, holding up four fingers.

"That's very impressive. Maybe I should watch how you do it since you're an expert."

"That's called cheating, and my mommy says cheating is bad."

And with that, he turned back to his own ornament, and everyone around him laughed, including the boy's mother who apologized profusely in between giggles.

He leaned over to Emily and said, "Man, I didn't realize the world of ornament-making was so cutthroat."

Emily laughed but didn't look up from her ornament. "We take Christmas very seriously in Bells."

Michael stared at his ornament and tried to think of the easiest thing he could do. He decided that presents were his best bet. How hard could it be to paint some squares? He dipped a paintbrush into the red paint and tried to paint a small, square present and found that, actually, it's quite difficult to paint a square on a spherical object. The shape was wonky, and when he tried to fix it with some gold outlining, it just got worse. He rotated the ornament and tried again, but the second attempt was even worse. He tried to paint a bow on top, but the paint started bleeding together, leading to a messy brown-ish mess. He added some red, green, and gold dots all over to try to help, but even the dots were misshapen and all different sizes. Setting the paintbrush down, he decided that additional attempts at correcting the problem were just making it worse, so he should quit while he was behind.

The little boy leaned over his arm to look at his ornament and said, "That's not very good."

His mother said, "Ben, that's not very nice."

Michael shrugged. "It's okay," he said with a laugh. "He's not wrong. Yours looks good, though."

Ben held up his ornament that had a simple red car drawn on it. "It's Hot Wheels. I asked Santa for it."

"Hope you get it."

"I will," Ben said confidently as he hopped off the stool and took his mom's hand. "Santa is really good at being Santa."

Michael waved as they walked off and turned to Emily laughing. "Did you see me get wrecked by this little kid?"

But when he faced her, he saw that she was gluing tiny rhinestones onto her ornament. She had painted a snowy scene complete with white glitter for the snowflakes, and she was placing the rhinestones in the center of each snowflake. The background was light blue, and the whole thing shimmered. It was stunning.

"I think you hustled me at ornament making," Michael said.

Emily laughed. "That is not a thing." She placed one last rhinestone and then set her paintbrush down. "There."

"Why are you so good at this?"

"Because I'm not a Grinch like you," she said with a smirk.

Michael rolled his eyes. "Seriously."

She shrugged. "It's kind of like decorating cookies, I guess. Same skillset."

"Well, clearly working in finance does not translate to anything artistic."

"Renee says you're a big reader. That's artistic in its own way."

"Words are much easier, and I'm not even the one writing them. Totally different."

"Fine, whatever you say."

Piper took both of the ornaments, sprayed them with some kind of quick-dry top coat, and boxed them up. When she handed them back over, Michael said to Emily, "You don't really expect me to put this on Darren and Renee's tree, do you?"

"It'll fit right in with their kids' ornaments from school."

"Ouch," Michael said, laughing, "low blow." After a moment of silence, he added, "You know, I'm kind of looking forward to Christmas this year. With the Moores, I mean."

"Yeah?"

He nodded. "It's the perfect idyllic family Christmas. When I got to town, the kids were building snowmen in the yard. It was a picture that should have been on a Christmas card. I've never had that, and I've missed Darren. We used to be so close. I'm really looking forward to a fun Christmas."

"Well, you're in the right place. If there's one thing Bells does right, it's Christmas."

Michael and Emily started wandering through the stalls again, and Michael noticed for the first time since he'd been in Bells how relaxed he felt. In Chicago, even when he wasn't working, he was thinking about work. The mental toll never really stopped, and he hadn't really been aware of how much that had been affecting him. Walking through Bells with a beautiful woman who made him laugh, looking at Christmas decorations, and holding an ugly ornament he'd made himself—well, he certainly preferred spending his time this way.

He didn't want to admit that Darren had been right about his workaholic ways, but already his short time in Bells had changed the way he thought about everything. When he had first told Naomi that he would enter the contest because he wanted to buy the bookstore, he'd felt a little like maybe he had lost his mind, but any trepidation that still lingered was evaporating from his very bones with every step he took through this Christmas market. He'd absolutely made the right decision, and he was more committed than ever to winning Deck the Shops if that was what he had to do to secure the bookstore and have a reason to stay in town.

He remembered that he needed to enter the contest before the tree lighting and checked his watch. He had time, but it was getting down to the wire, and he was totally lost in this maze.

"Emily," he said, "do you know where the entry table is for Deck the Shops?"

"It's over here. Why?"

"I'm entering," he said.

Emily stopped in her tracks. "How? I mean, with what business? Did you buy a business while I was making an ornament?"

He chuckled. "No. I was talking to Naomi at Something Worth Reading. She wants to sell, but she's kind of picky about who she's willing to sell to. She won't sell it to me unless I can prove that I'll take care of it the way she wants."

"So you suggested entering the contest?"

"It was her idea, actually."

"Wow."

"Is everything all right?"

Emily shook her head suddenly as if trying to focus after spacing out. "Yeah, totally. Sorry, you just caught me off-guard. The table is right over here."

He followed Emily to a booth where one woman was seated, and she wore an American flag pin and a nametag that read "Mayor Laura Rayburn."

"Well, hello there, Emily," the mayor said. "Lovely to see you."

"You, too," Emily answered. "This is Michael. He's staying with the Moores over Christmas."

"I'm Laura," she said, shaking his hand. "Lovely to meet you."

"You as well. I'm actually here to enter the contest."

"Really?"

"I'm sorry, I wasn't even totally sure I was allowed to enter. I don't live here. Well, not yet, anyway. I'm hoping to make the move to Bells."

"Well, we'd be happy to have you," she said. "But you do need to enter a Bells business to qualify."

Michael nodded. "I'm entering on behalf of Something Worth Reading."

Laura snapped her fingers. "Ah, you're the young man Naomi told me about. She said I should be expecting an entry from you. Well, just grab a form and fill it out with your information."

Emily then picked up an entry form. As she passed it over to Michael, the mayor said, "Oh, I assume you're here to enter Sweet Treats?"

Michael said, "Oh, actually I—"

"Yes, I am," Emily said, and Michael hardly knew what to say.

"Oh my," Laura said, "well, Michael, you've got some stiff competition, then. Sweet Treats is the reigning champion. In fact, they've won more than any other business in town." To Emily, she said, "Your grandmother has that special touch."

"Actually," Emily said, "I'm entering it this year. My grandparents handed over the reins for this round of Deck the Shops."

"Very exciting," Laura said, clapping her hands together, but Michael was having a little trouble focusing on her or the entry form. He couldn't stop staring at Emily as she filled out the form.

Darren had told him that there was a business in town that was tough to beat, but he'd neglected to tell him it was Emily's bakery. She'd mentioned having an opportunity to prove herself to her grandparents, but he hadn't connected the dots. Now, he didn't know what to think. Emily's whole demeanor had shifted when he had mentioned entering the contest. Was she angry with him? Did she resent him? Was he nothing more than competition to her now? Michael had to wonder how this would play out now. He needed to win to convince Naomi, but was winning to be able to stay in Bells worth it if he alienated Emily, a very big factor in his desire to move to Bells? Did she have to win to get what she wanted, too?

They both handed their entry forms to Laura at the same time, and she took them with a big smile. "Good luck to you both, and merry Christmas!"

"Merry Christmas," they both echoed, then walked in the direction of the big Christmas tree in the center of downtown. It was to be lit in a few minutes. Michael had been looking forward to the lighting—perhaps to share a romantic moment with Emily—but there was an awkward tension now.

"So," Emily said, a hint of apprehension in her voice, "I didn't realize you were entering."

Michael rubbed the back of his neck. "Yeah, I didn't really know either, but it's what Naomi wanted to convince her to sell to me."

"You're that serious about staying in Bells?"

He nodded. "I think so, yeah. I don't have a reason to go back to Chicago. And I like it here. Obviously, Darren and I are friends, but I like the people I've met here. I like—"

"That's great," she cut him off. "Well, good luck, then."

She jutted out her hand for a handshake, and Michael reluctantly reciprocated. Her hand was warm on his, but it didn't feel the way it had when she had led him through the market to the ornament stall—this touch lacked spark.

Michael wanted to say more—what he should say, he wasn't sure, but he wanted to fill the void—but the mayor took a microphone hooked up to a small sound system and makeshift stage in front of the tree. The whole town, as if sensing her presence, hushed and turned attention to her, so Michael had no choice but to do the same.

"Good evening, and merry Christmas!" the mayor said cheerfully, and everyone applauded. "We're so excited for our forty-third annual tree lighting ceremony. As you all know, this also marks the end of the official entry period for Deck the Shops. We will issue the event schedule the day after tomorrow. Best of luck to all of our entries! We can't wait to see what you all come up with this holiday season.

"And now, without further ado, let's officially kick off the Christmas season with the lighting of the tree. Countdown with me."

The whole town echoed a countdown starting from five, and when the mayor pressed the ceremonial button, the tree illuminated, and Michael thought that it was the most beautiful tree he'd ever seen. Chicago had a much larger, much grander Christmas tree they lit every year, but it lacked—well, Michael wasn't even exactly sure what it lacked. Heart, maybe? It was beautiful and immaculate, but just like the Christmas trees and decorations in his own home growing up, it was sterile and impersonal. This tree had paper snowflakes made by the different elementary classes at the local schools and charity opportunities and large red and green ball decorations that Darren said had been used on this tree since the first lighting forty-three years ago. And the community gathered around it felt friendly and familiar even though he knew almost no one here, unlike Chicago where he still knew no one and yet felt left out.

There was absolutely no denying it now: Michael was staying in Bells one way or another, and if Deck the Shops was his ticket to accomplishing that, then so be it. He glanced over at Emily, whose eyes were sparkling under the glistening lights that twinkled on the tree, and smiled at how lovely she looked smiling up at the tree. He was pretty sure he needed to win this contest to get the bookstore, but she also had her own reasons for wanting to win. He only hoped that she wouldn't be upset with him if he beat her.

13

Emily

Emily took the last batch of cookies out of the oven and let out a contented sigh when she set the tray down and rested her oven mitt-clad hands on her hips. They looked great. She'd intentionally made this batch last since they didn't need time to cool for icing, and honestly, they tasted better warm. Now that she'd finished all of the snickerdoodles, she had a great array. She'd spent days making different varieties of classic cookies for her "tasting party" as she was calling it. She'd invited some of her friends over to try some of her cookie and coffee ideas for the pop-up. She'd made different versions of snickerdoodles, sugar cookies, gingerbread, chocolate chip, crinkle cookies, linzer cookies, pinwheel cookies, and she'd even had a chance to knock out a few cupcakes as well. She was still convinced that she was right about selling cupcakes. She hoped that she'd maybe even sell out of cupcakes at the event, proving to her grandfather that people prefer cupcakes over slices of cake.

Her doorbell rang, so she ran over to answer, bumping into the coffee table she'd moved earlier. Her apartment wasn't ridiculously small, and it had two bedrooms, but the living room area was fairly little and not really conducive to having groups of people over, but Emily really didn't mind most of the time. She rented the apartment above the bakery, so it was extremely convenient. Her grandparents had lived in this apartment when they first got married and started the bakery, but eventually they moved out, and it had been rented out here and there by their landlord. She was grateful to him for doing some renovations in the meantime which meant that she had moved into an almost completely renovated space and was certainly not paying what it was worth in rent. One day, she'd get a house, but for now, this was a comfortable space for her.

She opened her front door, and Bella and Renee were outside smiling. "Come on in, guys," she said, gesturing for them to enter.

Renee handed her some flowers. "For our master baker and host."

Emily laughed and took the bouquet. "You're so sweet."

"So who else is coming?" Bella asked as she took off her jacket and hung it by the door.

"The two of you and Piper. She's coming from work, so she might be a few minutes late. Come on over and see what I made."

Emily stuck the bouquet in a vase while Bella and Renee admired the cookies and talked about how pretty they were.

"Do I remember correctly," Renee said, "that you're making drinks, too?"

"Yes. Coffee, hot cocoa, and some different kinds of lattes."

"Ooh, perfect," Bella said as she hopped up onto a barstool at the kitchen island. "You know I love any kind of hot cocoa. Hit me."

Emily poured two of the same drink flights she had made for her grandparents and laid out the cookie trays on the island so they could grab whatever they wanted.

After taking a sip from the mocha, Bella said, "Wow, this is really good."

"Thanks," Emily said. "Michael liked it, too."

"Michael?" Renee and Bella said simultaneously, both wiggling their eyebrows suggestively and lilting their voices.

Shoot.

"Is that hot diner guy?" Bella asked.

"Wait," Renee said, "why is Michael 'hot diner guy'?"

"Because he asked Emily on a date and he's hot."

Emily tried to interject. "Guys—"

"Now that you mention it, he is pretty good looking."

"Right," Bella said. "He asked her out for coffee at the bakery."

"Guys—"

"Hmm," Renee mumbled, as if Emily hadn't tried to say anything. "Well, he'll have to do better than that next time. Emily works at the bakery. That's not a date."

"It's a start."

Emily waved her arms in their faces. "You both are getting way too ahead of yourselves. He doesn't even live here. He lives in Chicago."

Renee snapped her fingers. "But he's thinking of moving here."

Bella added, "And he's got a stable job."

"That he quit," Emily said. "He wants to buy Something Worth Reading."

"That's fantastic," Bella said around a mouthful of red velvet cupcake with matcha icing. "That's like something out of a Hallmark movie."

"Oh my goodness, Bella, you're so right," Renee said, then spread her arms wide above her head as if displaying a marquee sign above her head. "'Big city guy moves to the small town and falls hopelessly in love with the local baker.' It's even Christmas season. It really is like a movie.

Emily pulled Renee's hands down. "Which is exactly why it's not a good idea to get all swept up in this insanity the two of you have created."

"I know he's only been here for a few days, but he seems like a really nice guy," Renee said.

"Had you never met him before?"

"I mean, he came to our wedding, and Darren kept in touch with him, but this is the first I've really gotten to know him. He bought some books for the boys, he brought us your dessert, which thank you, by the way," Renee said, and Emily smiled. "He's going to let the boys help him pick Christmas decorations, and he hung the Christmas tree lights on our roof that Darren hates doing because he's scared of heights. He's nice to have around. He pays attention, notices the little things." Renee laughed. "Actually, he kind of reminds me of you in that way."

"That's so true," Bella said. "I don't know how you remember the favorite dessert of everyone in town."

Renee added, "You both seem to have a talent for really seeing people in a unique way."

Emily fidgeted, swirling the cinnamon stick she held in her hand through her hot cocoa which was lukewarm at this point. That had been the problem with Noah, hadn't it? Noah never noticed anything. Noah hadn't noticed when Emily was stressed over her parents moving the Florida, and he hadn't really listened when she had told him her ideas for the bakery and wondered how she'd convince her grandparents. And he definitely hadn't noticed the months she'd spent thinking he was going to propose after she had found a small jewelry box in one of the drawers at his house only to discover that they were earrings he gave her for her birthday—a day late.

Noah had never seemed to understand why Emily invested so much energy and commitment into the bakery. *It's just a job*, he used to say, but to Emily, Sweet Treats was so much more than that. Sweet Treats was her life, her passion—after all, she'd given up on a whole relationship to put it first.

And it still came first. Hot diner guy didn't change that.

"I just don't see the point in getting involved in something that could go nowhere. He might not buy the bookstore, or Naomi might not sell. And what if he did? I hardly know anything about him. Besides, right now, I have to focus on winning Deck the Shops."

"Speaking of," Bella said, pointing at the half-eaten cupcake in front of her, "we've got to talk about whatever this is."

Emily's heart sank. "You don't like it?"

"I like the cupcake, and I like the icing, but the combination—it's throwing me off."

"Really?"

Renee nodded. "I think red velvet and matcha just don't go together."

Emily's elbows hit the island counter, and she let her head fall into her hands. "Ugh. I was trying to be Christmas-y. You know, red and green?"

Bella said, "I think red and green flavors just don't go together."

"What about a matcha cupcake and a red velvet cupcake?" Renee asked. "Separately, I mean."

"Every bakery in the country has that. I'm trying to do something different. I'll never sway my grandparents or the Deck the Shops judges with something run-of-the-mill."

Renee seemed about to say something, but a knock on the door interrupted, so Emily went to answer it. Mia walked in, looking flustered.

"So sorry I'm late," she said, shedding her coat and kicking her boots off by the door. "I got stuck training the new guy, so it's been a crazy day. Oh, it smells great in here, and I am dying for one of your sugar cookies."

Well come on in," Emily said.

Mia hugged Renee and Bella and headed straight for the kitchen counter to eye the cookies. She seemed to hesitate, and Emily was surprised: Mia never met a cookie she didn't like.

"Where are the sugar cookies?" Mia asked.

"Right here," Emily said, pointing to the array she'd laid out.

Mia frowned. "These are sugar cookies? They look different."

She picked up a green one decorated like a Christmas wreath and bit into it as Emily said, "I'm trying some new recipes. I want to be different, stand out."

Mia grimaced. "Emily, you know I love you and your food, but this is not great."

Emily's shoulders sank in disappointment. "Really?"

Mia nodded. "Is it pistachio flavored?"

"Yes," Emily said. "Don't you like pistachio?"

"Well, sure, but not in a sugar cookie. At Christmas, I just want to eat a plain, old-fashioned sugar cookie with too much icing."

"Yes, that's it, Piper," Renee said. "It doesn't taste traditional."

Emily slumped onto a barstool. "But that's the point. I'm trying to be innovative and creative."

Mia said, "I just think that, at Christmas, people really want the flavors they're used to. Part of the Christmas season is the food."

"It's nostalgic," Renee added.

"Exactly."

Emily sighed. "Maybe my grandparents are right. Maybe my ideas for the bakery are all wrong."

"No, I don't think that's it," Bella said. "I think you're just pushing yourself too hard, trying to be too different. You're an excellent baker. I think you just need to trust yourself and your skills a little more."

"I have to do something really good, really interesting, if I'm going to win, and I have to win."

Bella rubbed her back. "You're putting way too much pressure on yourself. You've got to relax a little. This competition is supposed to be fun."

"I've just got too much riding on Deck the Shops this time. I need it to work."

"What about Michael?" Renee said. "He's entering, too."

"Wait," Mia said, "who is Michael?"

"Hot diner guy," Bella said.

Emily covered her face with her hands. "Oh my gosh, you have got to stop calling him that."

Renee said, "He's staying with us for the holidays. He's a college friend of Darren's. He's from Chicago, but he seems to have taken a liking to Bells, especially Emily."

"Has he, now?" Mia said, raising her eyebrows suggestively.

"He's entering Something Worth Reading in the competition," Renee continued. "He's trying to buy it."

"So you're trying to beat him?" Mia asked.

"Well, no—"

"Ah, so you want him to win so he'll stay?"

"No, no. You guys are twisting it. I want to win. That doesn't change anything that may or may not be happening with Michael."

"If you say so," Bella said. "But I definitely think he likes you, and based on how red you are right now, I think you like him, too."

Mia held up a gingerbread cookie. "And this is delicious, for the record."

Emily sighed. "That's just a plain gingerbread cookie."

"Exactly."

Mia and Bella started hitting Renee up for information about Michael, and while Emily was half listening, she mostly stared at her cookie spread, despairing over what a failure this attempt had been. She couldn't win with cookies that weren't popular, but she also knew that she wouldn't win with unoriginal ideas either. She had to figure out a way to be creative without losing her target audience.

She also didn't know how to feel about the fact that for her to win the contest, Michael would have to lose, potentially losing his chance at buying the bookstore and staying in Bells. She knew enough to know that she didn't want him to leave town anymore.

This tasting had been a wakeup call in more ways than one.

14

Michael

Michael watched as Darren's kids ran down the aisles of Paint & Pine excitedly. He was looking for some Christmas decorations that he could use for the pop-up. Naomi had put up a few decorations, but he thought that this event needed more. Plus, he wanted to have some decorations that he'd put out just for the event itself to make it look special.

The problem was that Christmas decorations weren't exactly his forte. Because his parents always hired someone to decorate their house, Michael had never done the traditional decorating activities that other kids did around Christmas. He'd never put up lighted reindeer in his front yard or hung hand-made ornaments on the tree. He wasn't even sure his mother had ever kept the ornaments he made in school.

But he did know beautiful Christmas decor when he saw it as his house always looked perfect. He liked the traditional, classy approach to Christmas decor, and he felt reasonably confident that it couldn't be that hard to put together something simple and elegant. But now, standing in the midst of several aisles of bright lights, tinsel, and velvet, he wasn't so sure.

Darren's older son Timothy ran up to him clutching a box of lights that alternated white, red, and green lights. "What about these?" he said.

Right on his tail, the younger Rhett appeared from around the corner holding a box of blue lights that he could hardly get his arms around. "I like these."

Timothy turned to his younger brother and said, "Blue lights aren't Christmasy."

"Sure they are," Rhett fired back.

"They are not." He held up his own box. "These are Christmasy."

"Then why is Mom's favorite song 'Blue Christmas,' huh?"

"She doesn't like it because of the word blue, genius. She just likes Elvis."

"What's an Elvis?"

"Okay, okay," Michael said, holding up his arms in between like a referee in a boxing match. "What about white lights?"

"White lights are boring, Mr. Michael," Timothy said, hands on his hips.

"Yeah, boring," Rhett echoed, placing his hands on his hips just as his older brother had done in that form of childhood sibling mimicry.

"Boring?" Michael said, feigning outrage. "How can Christmas lights be boring?"

"They can't all be the same color," Rhett said.

"Then your blue lights are out," Timothy said.

"No, they're not because blue isn't a boring color like white."

Michael grabbed some garland from the shelf behind him. "What if we add this garland with the red holly?"

Both boys studied it carefully, and finally, Timothy said, "I guess so. But I don't know if I like it."

"Yeah," Rhett echoed again, "I don't know if I like it."

Michael heard a laugh behind him that someone had clearly tried to prevent and then coughed to try to disguise it. When he turned around, he saw Emily covering her mouth, her cheeks betraying a tinge of pink.

"I'm surrounded by critics," he said, rolling his eyes and flinging his arms out by his sides dramatically.

"I'm so sorry," Emily said, still suppressing a laugh. "I didn't mean to laugh, but it sounds like you've got a lot on your hands."

"My mistake for asking for decorating help from little boys."

"I'm not little," Rhett shouted. "I'm this many," he said as he held up nine fingers.

"Of course," Michael said. "Clearly I was mistaken."

Emily smiled and said, "Have a sudden need to decorate your room at the Moores' or something?"

Michael couldn't help but smile. How was it that Emily always made him smile? There was something about her directness or her wry humor that always made him happy, and he hadn't met someone who made him that happy in a long time. "No. I'm trying to pick out some decorations for Something Worth Reading. For the pop-up."

"Ah," Emily said, nodding slowly. "Well, I can see it's going well."

Michael sighed. "Any chance you'd help me?"

"Well—"

"Clearly I'm hopeless," Michael said when it seemed like Emily might shut him down. He was just hoping for an excuse to keep talking to her. "We obviously need a lot of help."

Emily laughed a little, and Michael was aware that his cheeks were starting to hurt from smiling constantly at her. He didn't mind.

"Sure," she said.

"Lead the way," he said, gesturing for her to take his cart.

Timothy and Rhett ran off ahead of them, and Emily started pushing the cart. "So, what kind of theme are you going for?"

Michael panicked. "Christmas decorations have to have themes?"

"Well, sure. Without a theme, you're just going to have Christmas chaos."

Michael laughed. "Well, that sounds like a theme to me."

"Not a cute one."

"Fair enough. What kind of theme do I want?"

"I don't know. What do you like?"

Michael looked around him at all of the different options and felt pretty overwhelmed. He didn't even know what a Christmas decoration theme should entail. Had his parents communicated a theme to the companies that did their decor? What was that theme?

"I don't know," Michael said, rubbing the back of his neck. "I guess I just like the classic look. You know, white lights, red holly, greenery. Nothing too crazy."

She nodded in a way he was used to seeing people nod in board rooms as business deals were closed and plans had to be made. She was all business, and she started plucking what seemed to be random things off of the shelves and dumping them in the cart.

"Classic, that's your theme," she said. "You like a traditional Christmas, right?"

"I guess so."

She held up a pink metal reindeer figurine that was at least three feet tall. With a straight face, she said, "So no pink metallic reindeer, then?"

He laughed harder than he had intended to. "Definitely not. What is this, the *Charlie Brown Christmas* tree lot?"

"Oh, I love that movie."

"Me, too."

She set the reindeer back on the shelf and patted its head before grabbing a similarly sized Santa figure—a realistic yet cartoon style one, not a weird metallic thing. "How about this? It would look great by the cash register or by the front door."

"I don't know. Isn't Santa kind of overdone?"

She gasped dramatically. "Overdone? Santa is classic."

"Trite is what some would say."

Timothy and Rhett ran back over, and Emily held up the Santa for them to see. "Boys, what do you think of the Santa figure here? Mr. Michael isn't sure it's a good idea."

The boys gasped in much the same way that Emily had. "You have to have Santa," Timothy said. "He's really important."

"I think you need a lot of Santas," Rhett said. "Like, just Santas everywhere."

Emily smirked at me. "I believe the jury has rendered their verdict."

"Fine, fine," he said, taking the Santa from Emily and placing it in the cart where it stared at him. "I'll bow to the peer pressure."

"Well, I think I've done all the damage I can do," Emily said with a smile, handing the cart off to Michael. "Just grab a few more boxes of white lights and maybe some poinsettias, and you should be good."

"Leaving?"

Emily nodded. "I've got to do my own decorating."

"And what's your theme?"

She flipped her dark hair over her shoulder as she walked away and said, "I guess you'll just have to come see it to find out."

As he watched her leave, Timothy poked his side and said, "Oooh, I think Mr. Michael likes Miss Emily."

"Likes her?" Rhett made a face.

"Like-likes her."

"All right, all right," Michael said, "settle down. We've got to finish our shopping."

He walked the aisles with Timothy and Rhett making jokes with each other, teasing each other, and suggesting increasingly outlandish Christmas decorations. The boys were totally off theme and coming up with the most wacky suggestions, but they'd gotten one thing right: Michael did like Emily, and she was all he could think about. Winning Deck the

Shops was important to him because he wanted to own a bookstore, but he was realizing more and more that maybe he wanted to win and buy the bookstore so that he could stay close to her also.

15

Emily

One of Emily's favorite Christmas traditions each year was visiting all of the local businesses on each of their pop-up event days. In past years, she had mostly just enjoyed the events, but this year, she would be sure to pay attention to how popular or successful each event was. She had to size up the competition.

Each business was assigned a different day—mostly the Thursdays-Sundays leading up to Christmas—to host their pop-up event, and the dates were never the same each year. Emily knew that the businesses that went toward the end typically did better because they were fresher in everyone's minds, and since it was a popular vote winner, that mattered whether or not people wanted to admit it. This year, Sweet Treats was the second to last event, and that was promising. Her event would be two days before final votes could be submitted, so she had a chance to make a big impression.

The problem was that the business with the coveted last date was Something Worth Reading. Michael would almost certainly benefit from that slot. Of course, Emily had no idea how good his chances were. She didn't even know what his idea was, and would Bells even accept an outsider as a winner? It might have been unfair, but there was a chance that Michael wouldn't win simply because he wasn't known. But when she thought about it, he was particularly charming...

Emily shook her head. Deck the Shops had to be her priority, and she couldn't let a guy—no matter how charming or handsome he was—distract her. Not again.

"There she is," Bella said as Emily walked up to the group. She was meeting Bella, Renee, and Mia so that they could attend together. These events were always more fun with friends, and it had become a kind of friends' tradition for them to attend together.

"Are we ready?" Emily asked, and they all nodded, heading inside of Evelyn's Floral Shop.

Evelyn's Floral Shop had been in Bells as long as Emily could remember. She could picture coming here as a little kid with her father and grandfather on Mother's Day to buy flowers for her mother and grandmother. It was a staple for every holiday or celebration of any kind. Evelyn was an old woman now, but she still entered Deck the Shops every year, and she never changed her concept. She didn't even care about winning; she just liked the tradition. Her event was always a popular one because she did a make-your-own-wreath event, and it was a fun, cost-effective way to get a wreath for the season. So Emily wasn't surprised when they walked in and found it crowded. She was surprised, however, to see Michael hovering in a corner of the shop looking more than a little uncomfortable.

Mia pointed at him. "Who's the new guy?"

Renee looked over. "Oh, that's Michael."

"That's Michael?" Mia said. "You never mentioned that Darren's college roommate was that good-looking."

"I wasn't exactly focused on his looks," Renee said with a laugh.

Bella slapped Emily's arm. "See? I told you he was 'hot diner guy.'"

"Oh my gosh, you guys are insane," Emily said. "He's going to hear you."

"He is not," Bella said.

"Michael," Renee called out, and any attempt Emily made to shush her was ignored. "Come here."

Michael walked over, looking more than a little startled, and smiled. "Hi ladies."

"Are you here alone?"

Michael nodded. "Is it obvious?"

"A little," Renee said. "Come on, join our table. We're short a person anyway."

Emily shot a look at Renee, but she shrugged sheepishly and without remorse. This didn't exactly make it easy to avoid Michael as she had intended.

The group of five—since they were now a group a five—claimed a table in the back. Evelyn always set up tables in a u-shape around all of the wreath-making supplies, but this year, it seemed she had gone a little overboard. Perhaps she was serious about winning this year.

Emily tried to avoid sitting next to Michael, but Renee and Bella seemed determined to orchestrate it, so she ended up to his left, and, comically, Michael was seated in the center of what was supposed to be a girls night.

Bella said, "What brings you out tonight?"

"I thought it made sense to check out the competition. So, how do these pop-up events work?"

Emily smirked and said, "Uh-uh, I'm not helping the competition."

"Ouch," Michael said with a laugh.

Renee said, "Each business creates an event that makes sense with the business they have. For example, tonight is wreath-making since we're at a floral shop."

"Makes sense," Michael said.

"The bar downtown does Christmas trivia night," Mia added.

Michael shifted his attention to me and smiled. "And what about the local bakery? What do they do?"

"Nice try."

He flashed a charming smile to the others. "Worth a shot."

"Okay everyone," Evelyn said, waving her arms, "take a seat if you haven't already. We've got plenty of room. We're going to get started. At each station, I have supplies for building your wreath. There are three different kinds of tree branches you can choose from, frames and twine to attach, and lots of decorations. You're welcome to use whatever you like, but make sure that everyone at your station gets a chance to choose."

Evelyn continued with some tips on weaving the branches just right, but Emily zoned out. In fact, she caught herself staring at Michael out of the corner of her eye, and she found that she didn't feel inclined to look away. Luckily, he was listening to Evelyn intently and didn't seem to notice.

Her thoughts drifted to Noah, and she hated that they did. Noah was the one she thought she'd marry. He checked all of the boxes: kind, attractive, funny, successful, and ambitious. His ambition had become the problem. He wanted more than a small town life in Tennessee. He had wanted to move to New York. When Emily had made it clear that she had no intention of being that far from family, he had reluctantly settled on Nashville, but even that was too far. They'd had no choice but to break up. They wanted such different things, and neither was willing to sacrifice that chosen lifestyle. It was nobody's fault, and yet, at the time, it had felt like Emily was to blame, that Emily was the stubborn, uncompromising one. But why shouldn't she stay committed to the life she wanted? Noah certainly had.

"Okay everyone," Evelyn said, interrupting Emily's thoughts. "Start building your wreaths!"

Absent-mindedly, Emily grabbed a few branches and started weaving. The problem with guys like Noah is that they weren't the bad guys, not the jerk ex-boyfriends at the start of the romance movie who leave the heroines jaded about love. No, guys like Noah were nice and doing everything right; they just didn't want to be *here* even when they thought they did. Noah spent months after their engagement trying to want to live in Bells, but he was always itching to return to the city. After a while, his visits to Bells became few and far between because it was just too difficult. They had both seen the writing on the walls and fought it for so long that they had broken their own hearts.

So maybe Michael thought he wanted to live in Bells for now. She didn't think he was lying about that, but she also knew it wouldn't last. Eventually, the walls of this small town would close in around him, and he'd be dying to leave it, too.

Shaking her head, Emily tried to refocus on the task at hand. She always bought a wreath from Evelyn for the bakery door, but she liked to make her own to hang on the door to her apartment. She didn't necessarily enjoy this tradition because she was good at it—in fact, wreath-making was not at all in her wheelhouse—but it was a nice, homey thing to do, and she liked the simplicity of it. So when she realized her branches were not totally symmetrical and that her holly berries were not sitting the way she had planned, she didn't mind. Some Christmas traditions were just about having fun. Not everything had to be perfect.

But when she glanced over at Michael making the most beautiful wreath she had ever seen, she couldn't stop the gasp that came out of her mouth.

"What?" Michael said without looking up.

Mia said, "Are you kidding me?"

Now, Michael did look up, confused. "What? What is it?"

"Your wreath," Renee said.

"What about it?"

"It's gorgeous," Bella said.

Mia wrinkled her nose. "No one told us we were inviting the wreath savant to sit with us."

Michael smiled just slightly. "So it looks okay?"

Emily stared intently at the perfectly woven, fluffy branches, the fake snow dusting he'd given them, the twirled gold and silver ribbons, and the perfect touches of red from expertly placed clusters of holly berries. It looked like the kind of wreath you ordered out of a catalog.

Emily said, "I think you've discovered a hidden talent."

He laughed. "If only I'd known back in college. I could have skipped the whole finance thing and done this instead."

Mia held up her frame that had branches sticking out every which way. "Any chance you do freelance work? Can I hire you to fix mine?"

"Might be beyond saving," Renee said, elbowing Mia playfully.

"How on earth did you get the berries to stay like that?" Emily said. "Mine either disappear entirely or stick out weirdly."

"Oh, let me show you," he said, scooting his chair closer to hers. "What you have to do," he said, picking the berries from her hand and delicately placing them, "is make sure the stem is stuck at an angle. If it's straight back, it's not stable. The angle keeps it from moving."

Emily tried to watch while he glued the berries in place to learn how he did it, but he was so close that she could smell his cologne and see the beginnings of a shadow growing along his jawline, and she found herself unable to take her eyes off of his face. There was something endearing about watching him now. She hadn't seen him so focused and serious like this, and even though the stakes were low at the wreath-making pop-up event, he handled the process with the utmost care. He squinted ever so slightly while he glued the berries, and she was drawn to the intensity in his hazel eyes.

When she finally did look away, she found that Renee, Bella, and Mia were all staring at her with variations of the same expression: smugness. She knew she was going to hear about this from them later, but for now, she rolled her eyes, and Mia jutted her head in Michael's direction.

"Like that," Michael said, putting down the glue gun and holding up Emily's wreath. "See?"

"It's perfect," Emily said, once again a little lost in his eyes which now seemed to sparkle as if he were smiling.

"I'm calling you the wreath master from now on," Bella said cheerfully, and everyone laughed.

"Hey, Michael," Renee said, "would you mind asking Evelyn for more gold ribbon? I think she's got some thinner ribbon, and I might have better luck with that than this big chunky one."

"Sure," Michael said and walked off to the other side of the store where Evelyn was helping someone with the fake snow spray.

As soon as he was out of earshot and distracted by Evelyn, all three women spun around on Emily.

"Oh my gosh," Bella said, "he so likes you."

"What, are we in high school?" Emily said.

"I told you," Renee said to Bella, then turned to Emily. "When he first got here, he used to talk about Chicago or his old job. Now, all he talks about is that bookstore and you."

Emily looked around nervously. Michael was still distracted, but he had gotten a hold of some gold ribbon. "He's going to hear you."

"Has he asked you out?" Mia asked.

"Of course not."

"Is that such a ridiculous question?"

"Yes. He doesn't live here."

"Yet," Renee said.

"And there's no reason to think he likes me."

Mia held up her comically tragic attempt at a wreath. "I'm just saying that I clearly needed the help with the wreath, but I'm not the one he offered to help."

"He offered because I asked him for help."

"And why did you do that?" Bella asked.

"Oh my goodness, all of you, stop talking."

Renee held up her hands in surrender. "Okay, okay. But seriously, what happens if he does ask you out? Are you going to say yes?"

Michael returned before Emily had a chance to answer, and she was grateful for his timing. She didn't know the answer to Renee's question because she hadn't allowed herself to think about it. Whether or not Michael wanted to ask her out wasn't a part of her equation. This season was about enjoying the Christmas activities, spending time with family, and winning Deck the Shops. There wasn't room for anything else.

Using the ribbon Michael obtained, Renee tied a final bow on her wreath, and everyone's wreath was done except for Piper's, and Mia had declared hers hopeless. They gathered their stuff, and just as the girls started to walk away, Michael said to Emily, "So, I hear the next one is at the diner. Some kind of retro theme?"

Emily was painfully aware of the fact that the others had stopped just far enough away to seem disconnected but close enough to eavesdrop. "Yes, Stella's Diner is hosting a '50s night dance."

"A dance, huh? That sounds fun."

"I think Stella's dance is my favorite pop-up event of the season every year."

He raised an eyebrow. "More than the Sweet Treats event?"

"That one is fun, but it's also busy and stressful."

"Fair enough. So you're going?"

"Of course."

"Would you like to go together?" Michael asked, and Emily noticed Bella's jaw drop behind him. "I mean, I know I crashed the party tonight, but I had fun, and I'm getting the sense that you're not really supposed to go to these events alone."

"They are definitely more fun with other people."

"And a dance—well, that just sounds like the kind of event that I should attend with someone. Maybe you'd humor me and dance with me?"

"Sure," Emily said before she even realized what she was saying. "I'd love to."

"Fantastic," Michael said, a big smile on his face, then held out his phone to her. "Would you mind giving me your number so I can text you to coordinate a time?"

Emily entered her number in his phone, wondering what on earth she was doing. Was she really giving this handsome man from Chicago whom she was competing against her number? Had she lost her mind?

"Just so you know," she said, "You'll have to dress up. For the theme, I mean. '50s attire is required."

"That's not at all surprising." He took his phone back and picked up his wreath. "I'll see you then, if not before for more desserts."

"Darren and Renee's kids might demand it."

He laughed. "See you later, Emily."

The second he was out the door, the others squealed.

"You've got a date," Bella said. "I told you."

"I guess that answers my questions about what you would say," said Renee.

"It's just the '50s dance," Emily said, rolling her eyes. "It's not that big of a deal."

"You know," Renee said, "it's not a bad thing. Just let yourself have a little fun."

The others nodded, and Emily tried to accept that. It was just fun. There was nothing wrong with going on a date and seeing what would come of it. She enjoyed spending time with Michael, and he'd made it clear that he was uncomfortable going to these events alone. That's all this was: company for the event. She could handle that. She was just going to have a little fun at the dance.

She glanced down at the perfectly placed berries glued in place by Michael on her wreath. Just for fun, she reminded herself.

16

Michael

It was late morning, and Michael had been at Something Worth Reading since 7 AM. He'd been spending time there almost every day lately, trying to get a feel for how this place ran, what were the routines, what could he expect from the clientele of Bells. He knew that if he had a shot at winning this contest that he would have to get to know not just the bookstore but the people of Bells really well. This wasn't the kind of place that accepted drastic change or outsiders easily, and he could only control one of those variables. He could only hope that Naomi's reputation and the fact that she entrusted him with the Deck the Shops event would carry some weight with everyone in this town.

Honestly, he was a little surprised at how much Naomi apparently trusted him. She'd handed him a set of keys, given him access to the computer system and all of the records, and she even left the store sometimes for extended periods of time while he was there. He'd become a kind of employee for the next few weeks, and it was apparent how ready Naomi was for retirement and a slower pace. He hoped that meant that his chances at buying were increasing.

The bookstore opened at 8 AM every day except for Sundays, and by 10:30, there was typically a lull until the lunch rush hit. Michael had already stocked the shelves with the small number of new books Naomi had ordered, cleaned up and straightened the tables, and dusted the leather bound collection. Everything looked neat, no one was in the store, and he took the opportunity to peruse the bookstore's financial records which Naomi had graciously allowed him to see. If he was going to buy a business, he wanted to make sure it was stable and didn't have any skeletons in the closet, so to speak. Some upgrades and minor fixes were fine, but he wasn't interested in a money pit.

He hadn't spent long looking through the paperwork, but so far, everything looked all right. There were some normal business expenses as well as some bigger ticket items—the roof had been redone last summer—but nothing seemed too bad or unusual. Michael was cheered by that. He would never buy a business without doing his due diligence, but he was really hoping that he wouldn't find any problems.

The only thing was that Naomi seemed to have incurred some expenses that didn't seem to add up. None of them were big, but over time, they'd taken a hit to her overall profit margin.

Just as he was about to dig deeper, Naomi walked in, and he was glad to see her. He hadn't seen her at all that day, and he was starting to wonder if she was all right.

"Well, hello there, Mr. Anderson," she said.

"I told you, you can call me Michael."

She flitted a hand without looking in his direction, fidgeting with the window blinds. "How is it going today?"

He shrugged. "A little slow."

"It'll pick up this week. The kids are out of school, and the parents will want to keep them busy."

"Since it's slow, would you mind if I asked you about some of these records you gave me?"

"Not at all," she said, sitting down on one of the armchairs at the front of the store with a groan.

"Are you okay?"

"Now, now, don't become one of those people who clutches their chest every time an old person makes a noise. I'm fine. I've just got creaky joints."

Michael suppressed a smile. Naomi certainly had a way about her. He sat in the opposite chair. "I was looking through the records over the last few years—"

"You got that far already?" She raised her eyebrows. "You work fast."

"I take my work very seriously. I noticed profits tend to dip in the summer, but I would think that would be a busier time for you with the kids out of school. Do you know why that is? Do people travel a lot?"

"No, but it's just a slow season. During the school year, the kids have required reading for school, and a lot of parents buy those books here, but it's getting harder and harder to compete with Amazon and the like."

"Have you considered partnering with the nearby schools? If you got the reading lists from the teachers in advance, you could order extras of those books and promote it as a one-stop-shop kind of deal. You could even sell the whole bundle at a discount and put the teacher's name and school's name on the order. That way, parents could just order everything up front based on their child's school."

She rubbed her chin, not particularly looking impressed but not put off either. "That's a very intriguing proposal."

"Obviously that would front load a lot of your sales for the year, but that would give you the income to do any repairs you would need to do before the winter gets too harsh. Speaking of, does Bells get much tourism?"

"Around Christmas, yes."

"You need a way to advertise that you're here to the tourists. I kind of accidentally stumbled upon the shop, but if I'd known it was here, I would have come by immediately. A lot of people love to read on vacation, and this place is cozy and warm. It's a perfect draw for the kind of people who would want to visit Bells."

Naomi leaned forward suddenly. "And what kind of people would want to visit Bells, do you think?"

Michael was aware that this was a test and that his answer was likely to sway Naomi's opinion of him, for better or worse. He'd have to choose his words carefully. "The kind of people who care about things and people that are real. People who want to visit small towns want authenticity, and that same desire will drive small business support."

She sat back in her chair, a small but smug smile on her face. Michael was pretty sure he'd passed the test. "Okay, I'm interested."

"The same would apply in the summer. Do Bells residents just not come here a lot in the summer?"

"No, they do, but my heart has always been for the kids. There's so much out there now competing for the attention of children. Books just don't carry as much clout as they used to."

"But they could. Books are magical as a kid."

She smiled again. "True, but the trick is getting kids to try. Once they do, most love reading, but it's hard to get a lot of kids in the door or to open a book. If I manage to get a reluctant kid to even touch a book, sometimes I just give it to them."

"For free? You mean you don't charge?"

She shook her head. "May not be the best business practice, but I care more about the kid reading than I do the fifteen dollars."

"But you could have both." Michael handed her the documents he'd printed earlier. "I was toying around with some ideas. A lot of businesses do punch cards, right? 'Buy ten ice cream cones, get the 11th free.' Why couldn't we do the same with books? And if your goal in the summers is to get kids reading, why not make some games or competitions out of it? Maybe kids get an extra entry into some kind of raffle prize for each book they read or make a Bingo card with types of books. The prizes wouldn't have to be big."

"You've really put in a lot of thought," she said, flipping through the papers.

"I can't take all of the credit. There was a bookstore near my house when I was a kid that did similar things, but I remember them so fondly."

"That's what matters." Abruptly, she slammed the papers on the coffee table and leaned in to stare directly into Michael's face. "So, here's the hard part: how do you get a kid to try a book?"

This was Michael's best idea, and he was both excited and anxious to pitch it to Naomi. "I firmly believe that people, including kids, who think that they don't like reading just haven't found the right book or the right genre yet."

"I'm in full agreement."

"So what about a 'book tasting'? We theme it like a restaurant tasting with different stations that are different genres. Kids get to sample different books in different genres to see what they like. There's no requirement to buy a book at the end of the night so there's no pressure. They just try different things, maybe chat with friends, and who knows? At the end of the night, they might find that they're still thinking about one particular story."

Naomi looked at him for a while, her expression completely unreadable, before she leaned in and said, "Now that sounds like a winning pop-up idea for Deck the Shops."

The elation Michael felt was palpable, and he didn't bother to hide the big smile that took over his face. That's what he was hoping, but he was still so unsure of his footing here in Bells. He thought it was a good idea, but he had no idea if it would land well here. Naomi's endorsement gave him the confidence boost he needed."

"Thank you," he said.

Naomi got up and started wandering the shelves, so he followed her. "Here's the thing, Michael. Like I said, I give you free rein to do whatever you like. You are welcome to any resources you might need, and you're welcome to use the bookstore's money to buy any supplies you need."

"What budget would you like me to stick to for Deck the Shops?"

She didn't answer him directly. "Do whatever you think is appropriate. Remember, I'm retiring for a reason. I'm too tired to bother with the event this year, and I'm selling this place come January, assuming I can find the right offer. If you want that right offer to be yours—"

"I do."

"—then act as if this shop is already yours. Run this event and this place exactly how you would. If it all succeeds and you can justify your choices, then that's what matters."

"You're really okay with my doing whatever I want with your store?"

"It's only my store for a few more weeks. I might be moving, but I at least want to see the beginnings of Something Worth Reading's new chapter."

Without so much as a glance or another word, she headed to the storage room and offices, leaving Michael alone again. He headed straight back to the computer to begin fleshing out these ideas. He didn't have much time until his Deck the Shops event.

This was all so different from what he had been doing in Chicago. This was still business and finance and numbers, but it was—fun? His work at Rothstein Investments had always felt like just that: work. He used to think that was normal. What was a job if not work? But his time at the bookstore felt totally different. He was still working just as hard—maybe harder, trying to prove himself to Naomi—but he left every day feeling exhilarated, not exhausted. He hadn't realized it until he'd quit and hopped a plane to Tennessee, but Rothstein had burned him out. His whole life had become about the job, and what for? All he had to show for the years he'd invested in that company was work experience on a resume, a line item on LinkedIn, and a resignation letter. At the end of the day, he'd been a nameless suit who was replaceable.

That was the other thing about working at the bookstore: it felt meaningful. His work at Rothstein was so impersonal, so sterile. He analyzed numbers and stocks trends, and sure, he was good at it, and the clients appreciated his skill, but what did that matter? Here, he was talking to Naomi about inspiring kids to want to read. It felt so much more worthwhile. His whole life, his parents had given him the impression that careers were about security, status, and success and nothing else, but here, he was looking at ways to build all three of those while still doing something he genuinely enjoyed. He couldn't believe how much his life had changed in the last few days just because he took the risk of quitting his job and visiting Darren and his family.

Naomi had said this was "Something Worth Reading's new chapter." He liked the sound of that, and he desperately wanted to be a part of that next chapter.

17

Emily

With every passing moment, Emily's mind was flip-flopping between thinking that agreeing to Michael's invitation to Stella's diner event for Deck the Shops was a good idea or a terrible one. At the time, it had felt like a friendly gesture, and Emily couldn't ignore that she really enjoyed spending time with Michael, but was she allowing herself to get too friendly with the competition? Could she really still think of Michael as just competition anymore?

She sighed and straightened the pink bow wrapped around her ponytail. It matched her Pink Ladies jacket perfectly. Stella's was hosting a '50s retro night, and since it was way too cold for a poodle skirt, she'd opted for a Pink Ladies jacket and black leather pants instead. It looked cute and was definitely on theme.

Stella's was a short walk from the diner, but the chill in the air was far too biting for just this thin costume jacket, so she grabbed her pink leather jacket—relishing at the fact that she got to wear the jacket she'd spent way too much money on last year—and black gloves on the way downstairs. She'd planned to meet Michael at the diner, so when she spotted him outside the bakery window, she came to a halt in surprise, then, catching herself, opened the locked door for him.

"Hey," he said with a smile, then flipped the collar of his black leather jacket and added, "How does this look? Am I on theme?"

Emily couldn't help but notice how well he pulled off the '50s greaser look. His typically sandy hair that was not usually styled was slicked back and darkened by hair gel, and he wore a leather jacket that was definitely nicer than anything a real greaser would have worn with dark wash jeans and black boots. The style was such a contrast to how he normally looked—coiffed and professional—but she found him just as attractive as always. Maybe even more so, she thought, because she really liked the way he was smiling at her.

"Nailed it," she said.

"You look perfect," he said, then gestured at her outfit. "I mean, the Pink Ladies jacket is spot-on."

She locked the bakery door behind them as they started walking. "I wear it pretty much every year."

"So the diner really does the same thing every year?"

Emily nodded. "Stella doesn't really care about winning. She just likes hosting retro night, so she puts up the same decorations every year and does the same event. She just likes a good party."

Michael laughed. "You know, I respect that. She knows what she likes."

"So, how are you feeling about Deck the Shops? Now that you've gotten to see some of the events, I mean."

He shrugged. "I don't know. Every event is so different, and it seems like everyone has a different goal, and not all of those goals are winning. It makes it hard to predict what will work."

"I know what you mean."

"Do you?" he said with a chuckle. "Apparently Sweet Treats has won more than any other business."

"Eh, people just like cookies."

"I think it's more than that. Your grandparents must have done something right all those years."

"That's why this whole thing is kind of risky for me. I should have this in the bag. No offense."

He smiled. "None taken."

"But I don't want to win with the same old thing. I want to win with my ideas, and if I don't, I'm not sure my grandparents will ever take me seriously."

"I don't know if that's true. From what you've told me about them and from what I've seen, they have a lot of respect for you."

"Sure, as their granddaughter, but I think that's still how they see me, not their adult general manager who wants to help the business succeed."

Michael seemed about to say something, but when they turned the corner, the music coming from the diner was suddenly loud, and he just started laughing. "I'm not sure what I was expecting, but it wasn't this."

"You thought small towns didn't know how to party, did you?"

He turned slightly pink. "That's not what I said."

Emily took his hand and pulled him toward the diner. "Come on, it's a blast."

The '50s music enveloped them as soon as they walked through the door, and a few people waved, but mostly, people were too busy dancing to notice that anyone had come in. There were so many traditions in Bells that were the same every year, and Emily loved them all, but the retro dance at the diner was among her favorites. It was always so much fun.

She was about to walk along the side of the diner to hang up her coat, but she realized she was still holding Michael's hand and was suddenly paralyzed with what to do about it. She'd just taken it to lead him in—she certainly hadn't planned to make it a thing, but now she didn't know how to stop it or if she even wanted to. He didn't seem to mind, but was he being polite? How long was it socially acceptable to hold the hand of a handsome stranger-turned-competitor-turned-friend?

"Wow," Michael said, and Emily was painfully aware of the fact that he had made no effort to drop her hand either. "People actually dance at this?"

"A diner throws a sock-hop, and you think people won't dance?"

He tugged at the collar of his white t-shirt. "I guess I didn't really think about it."

Emily put her free hand on her hip. "Michael Anderson, do you not like dancing?"

"It's not that I don't like it," he stammered. "It's just that I'm not very good at it."

"How is that even possible? I thought your parents threw big parties all the time. No dancing?"

He rolled his eyes. "Sure, but I don't think a Viennese waltz is going to help me right now."

"Homecomings? Proms?"

He shook his head. "Never went."

"Ugh," Emily said, a smile spreading on her face. "You've suddenly become very boring."

"That seems a little unfair."

"Come on," she said, taking the fact that she was still holding his hand as an opportunity to draw him to the makeshift dance floor. "'50s dancing is not hard."

"Fine, but remember that you brought this on yourself."

Emily tried to lead Michael through a few simple dances—jitterbug, hand jive, twist—but somehow he had actually downplayed his lack of skill. Emily actually found it kind of endearing to witness his abysmal dancing skills. She'd dated the kind of men who thought that dancing was enough to sweep a woman off her feet, and while it was nice, it wasn't the flex they often thought it was when they didn't have a romantic bone in their bodies.

Dancing with men like that always felt like interrupting a performance, and she didn't like to think of romance that way, something so one-sided. Michael's poor dancing made it glaringly obvious that he was not trying to show off for her, and she really liked that. He was so authentic even in his insecurities.

When he tripped for at least the fifth time, he started chuckling in a way that made her cheeks feel warm. "I think I'm hopeless."

Emily stroked her chin as if thinking deeply. "I think so."

The music shifted to a slower song, and Emily assumed that meant they would take a break, maybe get some food, so she was surprised when Michael took her hand and said, "Oh, thank goodness, a slow song. I can handle that. Dance with me?"

As an answer, Emily found herself moving toward him, and she placed her other hand on his shoulder. He placed a hand on the small of her back, but when he pulled her a little closer to him, Emily wondered if the blush she felt rising in her cheeks was visible. If it was, Michael had certainly noticed as he hadn't taken his eyes off of her.

"You're much better at this," Emily said, then silently berated herself for sounding so cheesy.

He let out a small laugh. "Glad I'm not a total trainwreck in the dancing department tonight."

"Well, now, I didn't say that."

He threw his head back, feigning as if deeply insulted. "Man, my ego is taking a beating tonight."

While laughing, Emily's eye caught on a couple dancing near them. She leaned in to Michael, lowered her voice, and said, "Do you see this couple next to us? Wearing the matching red outfits?"

He glanced over. "Yeah."

"That's Ruth and Ken Berens. They've been married for fifty-three years."

"Oh, wow."

Emily nodded. "He's a veteran, and she was a teacher for forty-something years before she retired. They always come to all of the Deck the Shops events, but this one is their favorite."

"Why is that?"

"They like to say that they remember the '50s. They were pretty young, but they both claim that this event is very authentic."

He smiled. "Somehow, I think there must be something about this event that is just fun and silliness and not exactly time period accurate."

"Don't say that to them." Emily watched them. Their dancing was more like shuffling, but they stared at each other the way you'd expect young lovers to gaze into each other's eyes. It was like they were seeing each other for the first time even thought he wore a red cable knit sweater that perfectly matched her red poodle skirt that she wore over thick leggings. "I think they just like dancing together. You know how when you're young people always ask what you want to be when you grow up?"

"Sure."

Emily jutted her head in their direction. "I want to be that, to have that. I don't think in terms of a career which I think is what most people expect as an answer to that kind of question. I want to be as happy with my life as Ruth and Ken."

Michael smiled. "That's beautiful."

She ducked her head down. "I know that was kind of corny."

"Not at all," he said softly but firmly. "I think it's a much more thoughtful answer to that question."

Emily knew the song that was playing, and she knew it was almost over. She found herself surprisingly sad to think that this dance was about to end, that Michael would let go of her hand, take his hand off her back, stop staring into her eyes and smiling. She wanted this moment to last forever.

"Well," she said, "I have to say, you are doing pretty well. I don't think you've stepped on anyone's feet this whole time."

"Is that so?" he said, but before she could answer, he abruptly spun her out, then back in again, then dipped her slightly before straightening back to the starting position. It was so fast that Emily felt as if she had to catch her breath after.

"Where did that come from?"

He shrugged. "I told you I had formal dance training, just not casual '50s dancing."

Humble about his limited skill—even more endearing.

The music stopped, and several people clapped. Michael let his hands fall to his sides, and Emily keenly felt the absence of their warmth.

"Well, I think we've earned a drink. How about you?"

She nodded and led him over to the apple cider. Stella made the best hot apple cider, and Emily looked forward to it all year. She poured two very full glasses and handed one to Michael who drank instantly.

"So you're not a Grinch about cider, then."

"I'm not a Grinch about hot chocolate either, you know. Just toppings."

"That's almost as bad."

"Well, hello there, you two." Emily turned to see her grandparents beside them drinking their own cups of cider. "You two seemed to have a blast on the dance floor," her grandmother said.

"So much so that we got thirsty for cider," Emily said. "Michael, these are my grandparents. This is Michael Anderson. He's Darren's friend."

"Oh yes," Grandma said, "I've heard so much about you. From Chicago, right?"

"Wow, news travels fast here," Michael said. "Lovely to meet you both."

"You as well," Grandpa said as he shook Michael's hand. "We're actually heading home for the night, but Emily, we wanted to nail down a date for game night. How is Sunday?"

"Perfect."

"Game night?" Michael asked.

Emily answered, "We have family game nights pretty regularly, but we like to have at least one Christmas themed one this time of year."

Michael smiled. "That is not the least bit surprising."

Emily elbowed him. "Hey, don't knock it 'til you try it."

Grandma smiled brightly. "Emily, that's a wonderful idea. Michael, why don't you join us for game night on Sunday?"

"Oh, I—"

"If you're free, of course."

"Grandma."

"I wouldn't want to intrude on your family time," Michael said.

"No intrusion at all," she added.

"You might as well," Grandpa added. "Eleanor always makes way too much food. We need more eaters."

Michael laughed. "Well, I can certainly help with that."

"So, you'll come?" Grandma asked.

"Sure. I'd love to."

Grandma clapped her hands together excitedly. "Oh, fantastic! I look forward to getting to know you on Sunday."

And with that, they strolled out, leaving Emily to wonder what on earth just happened. Had her grandmother invited Michael over because she saw them dancing together and assumed they were romantically involved? Emily found herself wondering if she really minded all that much if that assumption were true.

She said to Michael, "I'm not sure if you know what you've gotten yourself into."

"What do you mean?"

"My grandparents are very competitive when it comes to game night. They show no mercy."

"It's game night. How hard can it be?"

She laughed. "Famous last words."

Michael downed the last of his cider and tossed the plastic cup in the nearby trash can before offering his hand to Emily who accepted without hesitation, then wondered if she should have hesitated. She definitely wanted to hold his hand again.

"Do you think you have it in you to brave another dance with me?"

"I think I'll risk it."

With a smile and a small twirl of Emily, Michael led her back to the dance floor. Emily admired Michael's smile as he stumbled through a few mediocre dance steps. She didn't exactly know where she and Michael stood—whether or not this was a date, whether or not feelings were reciprocated, whether or not either of them was looking for something serious, whether or not it was a good idea to date the competition—but she did know that she would happily dance with Michael for as long as he wanted if it meant feeling his hand wrapped around hers and staring into those brown eyes.

18

Michael

Michael was oddly surprised by how nervous he felt walking up to the front door of Emily's grandparents' house. In the past couple of weeks, he'd impulsively quit his job, hopped a plane to the middle of nowhere Tennessee, entered some crazy contest to convince an elderly woman to sell him her business, and yet somehow, two kindly people welcoming him into their home—offering him a chance to spend time with the woman he was hopelessly falling for—was the most intimidating thing he'd experienced in a long time.

He didn't "do" family get togethers—not like this, anyway. His childhood was one of stuffy holiday events, and the most he ever saw his parents was when they were hosting some elegant gala. Truth be told, he probably saw the housekeeper more than his own parents. So what was the protocol for events like this? Were they casual? Serious? He'd been told it was a game night, but how did he know that this wasn't some kind of "meet-the-parents" situation since Emily was so close to them?

Michael huffed and adjusted the collar of his shirt. He was being ridiculous. Emily's grandparents were perfectly nice, and he had no reason to think that tonight was going to be anything but fun. He had to pull himself together.

Their house was quaint—there really was no other word for it. It was a charming cottage tucked back a ways from the main street so that he imagined it must be somewhat difficult to spot the rest of the year. Tonight, however, it was decked out in all white lights. He appreciated the classical approach to Christmas decor and inferred that Emily had probably deemed it "boring." It made him smile to picture that argument.

Before he could talk himself out of it, he knocked on the door. When Frank and Eleanor opened the door wearing matching hideously ugly Christmas sweaters, Frank frowned.

"Party foul!" he shouted.

"What?" Michael asked.

"Emily," Frank shouted inside. "This guy you invited is a real party pooper."

"Grandma invited him, not me," Emily shouted from inside. Michael could feel sweat forming on the back of his neck, but when Emily poked her head in between Frank and the door frame, her smile was enough to calm his nerves. "I told you to wear an ugly Christmas sweater."

Michael smiled sheepishly. "I thought you were kidding."

Emily pointed at her own blue sweater which had the *Peanuts* characters singing around a metallic Christmas tree. "Definitely not."

"Oh, we never kid about ugly Christmas sweaters," Eleanor said. "Come on in, we have plenty of extras."

Frank huffed, but Eleanor gently took his hand and led him inside and down the hallway. When she opened the door to reveal a spare room being used exclusively for holiday decorations, Michael failed at stifling a laugh.

Eleanor smiled. "We're not crazy, you know. We just like Christmas a lot."

"I'm sorry, I didn't mean to laugh." He looked at the wall of industrial shelving that all held bins labeled things like "decorations," "lights," "nutcrackers," and the hooks that held multiple wreaths and garland. "I just didn't know people stored this much holiday decor. This is all for Christmas?"

Eleanor nodded as she popped the lid on a bin labeled "Christmas sweaters"—of course. "Where did your family store your Christmas decorations? The attic? Basement?

"I'm not sure we stored it anywhere, honestly. My parents always hired a company to decorate. I don't think we actually owned any of that stuff."

Something flashed across Eleanor's face, too quickly for Michael to identify it, and she smiled elegantly to disguise it. "I suppose we're pack rats, but we're too sentimental to give anything up. Fortunately for you, that includes our sweater collection. Unfortunately for you, you're taller than my husband, and I doubt any of mine or Emily's would fit you, so you'll just have to make do with one of Frank's."

She dug through the bin, muttering as she looked at the size tags, periodically holding one up in front of Michael and squinting before dumping it and continuing the search. Michael let his eyes wander more around the room, landing on some family Christmas portraits from over the years. They were framed and labeled by the year, hung on the wall in chronological order. He started with this year's and worked backwards, smiling at each one. It seemed the family had tried to pick a theme each year. This year had been "winter wonderland," and they all wore light blue sweaters which looked so nice in front of the white snow. Last year, Frank and Eleanor dressed as Santa and Mrs. Claus, and Emily was an elf. A few years ago, they all donned green and did a Grinch theme.

Eleanor walked up beside him and pointed to a picture from when Emily was a child. "This one is my favorite. We did *The Nutcracker.*" A childhood Emily wore a ballerina leotard and tutu, and her grandparents and who Michael assumed were her parents were dressed as nutcrackers. Michael smiled at the way her smile still looked the same.

"They're beautiful," Michael said. "All of them."

"Did your family do portraits at Christmas?"

He nodded. "But they were always so formal. I think my father wore a suit in every one. Are these Emily's parents?"

"Yes, my daughter Helen and her husband Patrick. They live in Florida now, so they can't always make it for the family photos, but they'll be here for Christmas."

"I'm sure you're looking forward to seeing them."

Eleanor smiled, and Michael found that if he looked carefully, he could see Emily's smile there. He wondered if she had ever noticed. "Very much so. They're so happy in Florida, but I still miss them. I'm very grateful that Emily is still so close."

Michael nodded, but he found himself at a loss for words. It was such a nice moment, and he feared disrupting it.

Eleanor found a way to break the silence as she held up a red sweater with a silly looking Rudolph on it. "It lights up, too."

Against his better judgment, Michael laughed hard. "It's what I get for ignoring my instructions, I guess."

"I'm afraid it might be a little small on you, but I think it's the best we've got."

Michael shrugged off his coat and peeled off the navy blue sweater he'd worn because he thought it looked nice and would give a good impression—boy, had he been wrong. He pulled the red polyester nightmare over the white button down shirt he was wearing and found that he struggled to get the sleeves on. It was definitely too small, and he almost worried that he would rip it, and then where would he stand on Frank's list? He shifted the sleeves slowly, Eleanor helped, and finally, the sweater was on, not uncomfortably small, but comically too short in the arms and the torso.

Eleanor covered the smile that was spreading on her face with her hand. "It's lovely."

"Oh, now you're just patronizing me."

Eleanor giggled and ushered him out of the room. When he turned the corner and Frank and Emily spotted him, they both burst out laughing. Eleanor attempted to hush them, but her efforts were futile.

"Now you fit in at Christmas game night," Frank said.

"Wait, wait," Emily said as she walked over and squeezed Rudolph's nose, illuminating the entire sweater. "Perfect."

Michael winced. "I was hoping you wouldn't know that it lights up."

"You thought I wouldn't know when an ugly Christmas sweater lights up? I've never been so insulted in my life."

"Okay, okay," Michael said, arms raised. "Just wait until we get the games going. I don't like to lose."

Frank squared up across from him, though the smirk on his face made him slightly less intimidating. "But you're on my turf now. Christmas games are my specialty."

"Well, we'll have to see about that."

Frank took the hand of his wife. "Fine. We play in teams. Adults versus kids."

"We're hardly kids, Grandpa," Emily said, rolling her eyes.

"In my house, you're kids. Now come on, grab some refreshments, and let's get going."

Frank scooted off to help Eleanor set up some games on the table while Emily led Michael over to the kitchen where the counter was covered with different cookies and pastries.

"Good news for you," Emily said. "Grandma made her famous cider, so you can drink that instead of your Grinchy version of hot cocoa."

Michael smiled. "Thank goodness. Is all of this from Sweet Treats?"

"Mostly," she said as she poured some hot cider that smelled delicious as it wafted over to him. "A few of these things we don't sell. Family recipes."

"Aren't family recipes exactly what you should be selling in a bakery?"

Emily laughed, but it came out more like a snort. "Try telling my grandpa that. What would you like?"

"Baker's choice."

Emily raised an eyebrow questioningly but grabbed a plate. "Okay, you asked for it. You're getting the works." She started loading up the plate, and Michael thought—with no regrets—about the stomachache he was sure to have later from the sugar. "Sorry about my grandparents, by the way," Emily said, her voice hushed. "They take game night very seriously, especially at Christmas."

"I don't mind."

Her eyebrow went up again. "Are you sure? Because you look ridiculous in that sweater."

"Pretty sure that's because this is a ridiculous sweater."

"Pretty sure it's because it's about three inches too short on you."

Michael shrugged. "Worried it'll distract you from winning?"

"You better hope not since we're on the same team. There," she said, handing him a plate piled with treats. "Ready?"

"You bet."

They started with Christmas themed charades, and Frank and Eleanor definitely beat them that round, but he and Emily did better with Pictionary. They'd split the rounds of "Name that Christmas Carol" and Christmas trivia, so it all came down to "Pin the Nose on Rudolph." They'd hung a large picture of Rudolph with target rings on the living room wall, and they each had a big, fluffy red ball with tape attached. Frank held the blindfold as he explained the rules.

"Okay, this one is for all the marbles. The team with the two closest noses wins. Loser takes out the trash."

"You're on," Michael said.

"Ladies first."

Eleanor started, getting her nose respectably close on Rudolph's neck. Emily followed, and hers was in the left antler. Frank got about as close as Emily, landing his nose on Rudolph's raised hoof.

"All right, Michael," Emily said. "It's all on you. You just have to get in the second ring, and we win."

"Is there any strategy to this?"

"None at all."

"Well," Frank said, "if you're planning on losing, there's no strategy."

"All right, all right, let's do this," Michael said.

Frank tied the blindfold on him, spun him three times, then nudged him forward. Michael had tried to make a mental note of the reindeer, but now he felt disoriented. He hoped he remembered where Rudolph's ears were and smashed the red nose against the wall. When he took off the blindfold and found that his nose hadn't actually landed on Rudolph's face at all and was instead almost off the poster itself, Frank cheered, and he and Emily groaned.

"Adults beat kids!" Frank said cheerfully. "I warned you. I am the Christmas game champion."

"I was foolish to think otherwise," Michael said. He jutted out his hand, and Frank shook it. "I bow to the master."

"I'm impressed," Frank said. "Even though you lost."

Michael laughed. "Point me in the way of your trash can."

He followed Frank to the kitchen while Emily stayed in the living room to help Eleanor clean up. Frank opened a cabinet under the sink and pulled out the trash can. Michael grabbed the bag and started reaching for stray trash on the counters.

"Well, son, I'm glad you could make it tonight," Frank said. "Despite your lack of ugly Christmas sweaters, you did well."

"Did I pass the test?"

"What test?"

"I don't know, it just feels like maybe this was a test."

Frank smiled and patted him on the back. "No test, son. Just some holiday fun. The can's around the back."

Michael hoisted the bag and went out the back door in search of the trash can. After he dumped it and turned back toward the steps, he found Emily leaning against the column.

"You didn't really have to take out the trash," she said.

"A bet's a bet. Besides, it's the least I could do."

Emily sat down on the steps, so Michael sat beside her. "I hope you didn't think tonight was too silly. My grandparents can be kind of embarrassing sometimes."

"Not at all. I had so much fun. I can hardly remember the last time I laughed as hard as I have tonight."

"Really?" Emily said, her voice betraying relief. "I was kind of afraid you'd never want anything to do with any of us after you saw my grandpa turn militant over Christmas charades."

"In all seriousness, I've never had a Christmas like this before. Christmas growing up was an event, and not a fun one. I knew my parents were kind of uptight, but I guess I didn't really think people did the things they do in Christmas movies. You know, decorate ornaments, build wreaths, sing carols, play Christmas games. I always kind of thought that was some Hallmark manufactured stuff."

"That's kind of depressing," Emily said, then turned red, her eyes widening. "I didn't mean it like that, I just—"

Michael laughed. "No, it's depressing. What I'm trying to say is that I've really enjoyed the way Bells does Christmas, the way your family does

Christmas. Thank you for inviting me. Or rather, thank you for not banishing me after your grandmother invited me."

"Well, you know how grandparents can be."

"Actually I don't. My father's parents died before I was born, and my mother's parents passed when I was really young. It was just me and my parents, and my parents I didn't see that often."

"I'm so sorry."

"It's not your fault."

Emily let the corners of her mouth turn up a little. "No, of course not, but I mean—I just can't picture life without my grandparents."

"Well, I'm glad to have been adopted by them for tonight."

"Happy to share."

Emily's words bounced around in his head. *You know how grandparents can be.* Michael didn't. He'd never really known them. He had used to think that you couldn't really miss something you'd never known, but tonight, with Frank and Eleanor, he realized just how wrong he'd been. He found himself missing something he'd never had in the first place, and he was shocked at the sharp feeling of longing. He felt he might have missed out on a fundamental part of life, of being human. He wondered if it was possible to make up for it now. He looked down at the ridiculous sweater he was wearing and smiled. Somehow, he felt that he could.

Michael looked up at the sky. It was a clear night, and the stars were shining brightly. Even though it was pretty late at night, the light they gave off along with the moon kept it from being totally pitch black outside.

"You know," Michael said, "I could swear there are more stars here than in Chicago."

"You can just see them better. Less smog, fewer city lights."

"If you say so. I think it's something about Bells. It's just nicer here."

"What's better about it?"

Michael turned to look at Emily, and she did the same. He found himself entranced by her the reflection of the Christmas lights sparkling in her eyes. He noticed a stray strand of hair caught on the frayed edge of the Christmas tree on her sweater, so he brushed it over her shoulder.

"You're here," he finally said. "That's what makes Bells better than anywhere else."

Emily smiled, but her gaze was fixed on his eyes. He allowed his eyes to flit down to her lips, and when he leaned in, he found that she did, too. He kept his hand on her shoulder. She smelled like the gingerbread cookies she'd been eating all night, and it made him smile.

He started to lean in further when the back door opened, and they both snapped back suddenly, startling Frank who was holding another trash bag.

"You missed one," Frank said, holding out the bag to Michael, who stood awkwardly and took it.

"Sorry about that."

"Emily, are you staying for the movie?"

She cleared her throat and stood. "Of course."

"Michael, you're welcome to stay. Eleanor wants to watch *A Christmas Carol*. Family tradition. Charles Dickens is one of her favorites."

Michael smiled as he tossed the second bag in the can. "Mine, too. I'd love to."

Frank nodded and headed inside, leaving him alone with Emily, but they couldn't seem to make their way back to the moment that was interrupted. Emily was flushed, and Michael struggled to ascertain if that was because of the almost kiss, her grandfather's interruption, or the chilly air outside. Likely, it was a combination.

"We should probably—"

"Right," he added.

She pointed at his sweater which was still flashing. "Better turn that off. Grandma takes movie night almost as seriously as Grandpa takes game night. Don't want to ruin it."

"I would never dare."

Emily took just one step toward him, squeezed Rudolph's nose until the sweater stopped blinking, then smiled. She seemed to hesitate, just for a moment, then walked back inside, holding the door for him to join her.

Michael smiled as he followed her inside the house and sat down on the couch next to her as the movie began. Eleanor handed each of them a mug of warm cider, and he relished the warmth on his hand, but more importantly, he cherished the feeling of this exact moment. He was sitting on the couch next to a beautiful girl, about to watch one of his favorite movies, drinking warm cider, and enjoying the silly bickering but affectionate glances between Frank and Eleanor. Michael had never dreamed that his life could be this perfect, but now that he'd had a taste of it, he was going to do whatever it took to ensure more moments like this in his future. And he knew he had to have another shot at that kiss.

19

Emily

Stepping off of the chair she'd been standing on, Emily looked up to admire her work. It had taken her nearly an hour to hang all of the snowflake lights from the ceiling—and several days to put up all of the other decorations—but she had finally finished, and she liked the ambiance.

She looked around the bakery and wondered if maybe she'd gone a bit overboard. She'd used all of the decorations her grandparents already had for Sweet Treats, but she'd spent more than a small amount on new ones, hoping to breathe life into a stale design. It was—well, for lack of a better word, busy. Her goal had been to make Sweet Treats like a winter wonderland, especially since kids were her target for the Deck the Shops event. She wanted that magical Christmas vibe, and while she felt sure she'd done enough to achieve it, she couldn't help but wonder how many ways her grandfather would criticize it for being too elaborate.

She broke down the rest of the boxes and stacked them to take to the dumpster. It was still slow for now, but her mid-morning rush was probably imminent, so she wanted to make sure she cleaned up after herself before customers came in.

As quickly as the thought occurred to her, she heard the bell chime over the front door. She was exceedingly happy to see that it was Michael who had walked in.

"Wow," he said, his eyes wide.

Emily put her hands on her hips. "I told you that I don't play around when it comes to Christmas."

He rubbed the back of his neck and chuckled. "That you did."

"Here for more pie?"

After he hung his coat on the coat rack by the door, Michael sat down on one of the stools at the counter. "No. You know what? Surprise me."

Emily raised an eyebrow. "You sure about that?"

"Absolutely. I'm feeling adventurous. And I'm positive you've put together some kind of special holiday menu, so I'm giving you free rein."

"Whoa, the power."

"Don't let it go to your head," he said with a smile. He smiled exactly the way he had the other night at her family's game night—the way he had smiled when she was certain they were about to kiss. She hadn't been able to stop thinking about that moment since it happened, and she found herself wishing constantly that they hadn't been interrupted.

"Any allergies?" she asked.

"None."

"Then I'll be right back."

Emily ducked into the back to decide what she should bring Michael but mostly because she needed a break from staring at that smile, that smile that made her desperately want to kiss him. That smile that made her forget about Noah and how he'd left and how she'd been convinced that Michael would do the same. Wasn't he putting a lot of effort into Deck the Shops so that he could stay here? Maybe he was different from Noah. Maybe he really did want to stay. He was best friends with Darren, and Darren was more than happy in Bells. That meant Michael could be the same, right?

She shook her head, reminding herself to focus on the task at hand. She grabbed one of the cupcakes she'd made last night and poured two cups of coffee. If Michael wanted to try something new, then he could at least sample one of her new menu ideas. She needed all the guinea pigs she could get before she tried to convince her grandfather of these ideas.

When she walked back into the main shop, she found Michael fidgeting with the gold garland that was wrapped around the edge of the counter.

He looked up, red in the face. "I might have knocked your garland down."

"Gosh, Michael," she said, rolling her eyes but smiling, "can't leave you alone for two seconds."

"Hey, it's not my fault. There's a ton of garland here. I barely touched it."

She glanced at the garland. "Okay, maybe I went a little bit overboard on the garland."

"Can I say something? I think you may have gone a little bit overboard in general."

"What do you mean? It's festive."

Michael gestured around the room. "But it's kind of a lot. What's your theme?"

"Bakery?"

He smiled. "No, that is your business. What is your Christmas theme?"

"You're the one who didn't have a theme."

"And you're the one who said I needed to."

"Deck the Shops doesn't technically require a theme."

Michael rolled his eyes. "Oh sure, you tell me that now."

"What's your problem with my decorations?"

"Your decorations are not cohesive."

"Sure they are. They're all Christmas decorations. That's cohesive in and of itself."

"Okay, but look at this." He hopped up and walked over to the booth wall. "You've got snowflakes here, and a lot of the decor is blue and silver. It's very 'winter wonderland.' But over here," he pointed to the counter, "everything is gold. And over there, everything is red and green."

"You have a problem with color?"

"And some of your decorations are little Santas and reindeers, but then you have trees here, and over there are random vintage red trucks."

"It's all Christmas related."

"It's just kind of a lot. It's honestly a little overwhelming to walk in here."

Emily rolled her eyes and sat on the counter. "You sound like my grandfather."

He sat on the stool next to her, and she was acutely aware of the fact that the bakery was empty, and he could have chosen to sit anywhere else, but he chose to be close to her. "I'm not trying to rain on your parade. I just think it could be more organized, unified, that's all."

"But I want that 'wow' factor, you know? I mean, you even said it when you walked in."

"That's because I was in shock."

"I just want to go really over the top, really extravagant. I'll need it if I'm going to beat—"

"Beat me?" he said with a smirk.

"Beat everyone. It's really important to me that I win. I've been decorating for days, and I've made so many new cupcakes and cookies that I think I'm losing the ability to taste sugar."

"That's dangerous. I think you need a new taste tester." He glanced down at the cupcake sitting next to her. "Is this one of them?"

Emily nodded. "The coffee, too. Both specialty holiday flavors."

"Well, let's see, then." He took a bite of the cupcake, looking pleased at first, but his brow furrowed. "It's good but—what is the flavor in the icing? I can't place it."

"Cranberry. Do you not like cranberry?"

"No, it's fine, but I don't think I was expecting a cranberry flavored cupcake."

"Cranberry is a classic Christmas flavor."

"Of course, but not a classic cupcake flavor."

"What about the coffee? It's peppermint white mocha."

Michael took a sip and smiled. "That's delicious."

"Great!"

"But it kind of clashes with the cupcake."

She threw her head back. "Ugh."

"Sorry, I don't mean to come in here and burst all your bubbles."

"No, it's fine. This is just exactly what my friends said. I threw a tasting party, and they said everything tasted like I was trying to hard."

Michael took her hand in his, and Emily's heart fluttered at the warmth from his hand. "You're an excellent baker. Everything I've gotten from you has been delicious. I think you just need to trust yourself a little more. The classic desserts are classics for a reason."

"But classic isn't going to win Deck the Shops."

"Who says?"

"The unofficial rules."

"Well, what did your friends say?"

"I made these cookie and drink flights, but they said they just wanted traditional flavors." She described each of the flights to Michael.

"Hmm. Maybe you just need to rethink the flights."

"How so?"

"The flight idea is good, but instead of four totally unique flavors, some of them are traditional?"

Emily twisted her mouth. Maybe that was the answer. She'd made this harder than it really needed to be. "What about a gingerbread flight? One gingerbread is normal, and the others are fun twists."

He snapped his fingers. "Yes, that's perfect. The same with the cupcakes and the coffee." He took another sip. "Because seriously, this coffee is really good."

"Thanks. I'll have to decide what to do about the cupcakes."

"What do you mean?"

"My grandfather doesn't want to sell them. He thinks they're too gimmicky."

"Well, I like your grandfather, but he's wrong on that one."

Emily spread her arms wide. "Thank you!"

He leaned in closer and smiled. "Now what's this I hear about a tasting party? Why wasn't I invited?"

She laughed. "I just had some of my friends over. I wanted their opinions on my dessert ideas for Deck the Shops."

"I'm offended. Are we not friends?"

"Are we?" Emily said, then immediately regretted being so forward. She found herself hoping that they were beginning to qualify as more than friends.

"If not, then my total criticism of your decorations and ideas is going to seem kind of rude."

She laughed. "I love the new flight idea. I wouldn't have thought of that without you."

"Happy to be of service."

He leaned in further, and his elbow brushed against her knee. There was no denying it now—she was definitely hoping they were more than friends. Bella and Mia and Renee were right: she had to let go of the past. Michael wasn't the same as every other guy. She had to learn to trust her heart again.

But just as before, the moment was interrupted by a customer walking through the door. It was Mr. Reynolds, the elderly man who lived near her grandparents, and he raised an eyebrow when he saw Emily sitting on the counter, so close to Michael.

Emily hopped off the counter quickly. "Your usual, Mr. Reynolds?"

"Thank you, dear," he said, shuffling off to his usual table by the window.

"Sorry," Emily said, "duty calls."

"No worries. Hey, do you usually go to this Christmas hockey game thing?"

Emily grabbed a croissant from the case. "Uh, of course. It's one of my favorite parts of the season."

Michael narrowed his eyes. "I'm starting to think everything is your favorite part of the season."

"Busted."

"Would you like to go with me? I love hockey, and since Darren is on one of the teams, I want to go, but I don't really want to go alone."

"Only know so many people in town?"

He smiled sweetly. "Well, no, but I'd like to go with you."

Emily had to force herself from smiling too wide. "I'd love to."

"Pick you up here?"

"Perfect."

He popped a lid on his coffee and stood, grabbing his coat. "It's a date."

As he walked out, Emily found that she was actually giddy, and it made her almost laugh at herself, but she couldn't deny how happy she felt. Michael had asked her out, and for the first time in a long time, she was really looking forward to a date.

20

Michael

The drive to the ice arena was a scenic one and not one Michael had made yet in his time in Bells. He pretty much hadn't left Darren's neighborhood or the downtown area, but this drive was nice. He'd never been somewhere with so much open land. He'd grown up surrounded by cityscapes, and even when his family went on vacation, they went to overly developed touristy areas. He'd thought it was strangely quiet at first, but he was beginning to realize that he didn't miss the constant noise.

Plus, Emily was sitting in the passenger seat next to him, and she made every experience better. It was like she was full of light, and her radiance lit up the world around her. He'd lived his whole life without knowing her, but now that he did, he couldn't imagine life without her. He felt certain the world would seem dim without her presence now.

He risked a glance at her, but she didn't even notice because she was busy belting "Santa Claus is Coming to Town" at the top of her lungs, slightly off key, but nonetheless charming. They were both wearing red sweaters—apparently the community hockey game was red vs. green, and since Darren was team red, they had both dressed to support him—but it didn't look nearly as good on him as it did on her. Her red lipstick was an exact match, and it was hard to keep his eyes on the road when he'd rather watch her lips as they smiled around the words of the Christmas carol.

He let out a small sigh. There was no denying it anymore—he had fallen hard for Emily. Initially, he had worried that the competition would drive a wedge between them, but they saw each other almost every day now, and this was definitely a date. He couldn't think of any other time that he had felt like this about a woman, and he was elated by the possibilities of staying in Bells, where Emily was, and running a bookstore. It was so close, he could taste it.

"Okay, party foul," Emily said, clicking the radio volume down. "When a Christmas song comes on, you have to sing along."

Michael laughed. "Oh, do I? Who made that rule?"

Straight-faced, Emily said, "I'm pretty sure it was Santa Claus himself, and you don't mess with Santa."

"Of course not. That would be ludicrous."

"Are you distracted by something?"

Yes, he thought. *By you, the way you smile, the sparkle in your eyes.* "No, sorry, I was just thinking I haven't been past downtown until now."

"There's not much to see," she said with a shrug. "There's a Walmart and the ice arena. Plus a gas station. That's about it for another several miles."

"So, how seriously do people take this hockey game?"

"Depends on what you mean. As I'm sure you already know from Deck the Shops, people can be pretty competitive in Bells."

"Are the teams any good?"

She chuckled. "Well, that's why I said it depends. They're not great, but the game is still entertaining. On Black Friday, the town does a draft to select players for the red and green teams, but Bells isn't exactly a hotbed of untapped hockey prodigies."

Michael turned into the parking lot for the ice arena and started looking for a spot. Emily wasn't kidding—the parking lot was packed. They were going to have to park pretty far away. "You know, I used to have season tickets to the Chicago Blackhawks."

"Used to?"

He nodded. "I don't really go to games all that often anymore, so I canceled it."

He parked, hopped out of the car, and opened Emily's door. She asked, "Why'd you stop going?"

"Too busy. Work kind of took over. I was always working overtime hours trying to get a promotion, but I didn't have any time to do anything but work."

"Did you at least get the promotion?"

He laughed loudly. "No. I actually quit my job over it."

"Really?"

He nodded as they walked toward the arena. "Yeah, that's why I first came to visit Darren. I got passed over for someone with way less experience. I just realized how little they valued me there. At first, I just thought I'd take a break, see Darren and Renee, and then apply for different jobs. Something Worth Reading and Bells in general just kind of fell out of the sky for me."

"Oh, wow. I had no idea." Something in her voice sounded a little sad to Michael, and he wondered which part of that exactly had concerned her.

He shrugged. "It's all right. Things work out the way they're supposed to, right?"

As soon as they walked in, Michael was struck by how loud it was. He had expected kind of a low turnout or a quiet community crowd, but the place was packed, and everyone was dancing to the pre-game music—which was, of course, Christmas music—and cheering.

Emily smiled at him. "Anything like a Blackhawks game?"

"Nothing like a Blackhawks game. It's so much better."

And it was. Michael had never had so much fun in his life, and not just at this hockey game. He couldn't think of a time in his entire life that he'd enjoyed as much as he had enjoyed these few days in Bells. Previously, he would have said that college at Northwestern was the highlight, but this was different. College had always felt a little bit like a temporary experimental phase of life, one not meant to be permanent but nonetheless one of those phases that felt obligatory to growing up. He'd loved college because he loved the classes and the activities and the freedom. Graduation had brought a harsh reality fraught with stress and billable hours and backstabbing competition. In Bells, he had been welcomed not just by an old friend but by the entire community. They'd invited him to join them at community events, into their homes for fun traditions, and even into their businesses. He'd never felt so connected, so happy, so seen.

"Come on," Emily said, taking him by the arm, a gesture that made him feel warm. "I think Renee is over there."

They sat down next to Renee who was sitting with some of the other wives of the red team's players. While watching the two teams warm up, he realized that Emily had been right: none of them were really any good. He laughed to himself at the realization. Maybe if he was still in Bells next year, he could join one of the teams. He'd played hockey as a kid all the way through high school. He was likely rusty, but it didn't look like that much mattered here.

He liked the idea of that, of still being in Bells next year to join the hockey scrimmage. That was definitely something that he wanted. It was the reason he'd asked Renee if she knew any realtors in the area. She had referred him to a friend of hers—because it seemed that everyone in Bells was friends with each other—so he had sent her an email. He had wondered if he was getting ahead of himself—after all, he hadn't even hosted his Deck the Shops event, much less won—but he had also started to think about what he would do if he didn't win and buy the bookstore. Would it matter? Was he intending to stay in Bells anyway? It felt right to stay, but the practical side of him that his parents had worked hard to shape screamed at the idea of moving somewhere without a job lined up.

The buzzer sounded, signaling the end of warm ups, and Michael took the opportunity to clear his mind. He couldn't think about any of that right now, didn't want to think about it. Right now, he was at a hockey game with Emily, and that was all that mattered.

After the anthem, the puck was dropped and gameplay started. Emily leaned over and said, "So the goalie on the green team, that's Hank. He's left-handed, and even though he's been the goalie for years, most of them regularly forget that his weak side is his right." She pointed at the forward for the red team who was currently skating the puck down the ice. "And that's Nehemiah. He and Darren are always on the same line. They've been playing hockey together since pee wee leagues."

"Wow, you really know your players, don't you?" Michael said.

She shrugged. "It's easy when you've known them all for so many years."

"Okay, honest question. Did you really enjoy growing up in such a small town? Like it never bothered you?"

"It really never bothered me," she said with a laugh. "Everything about Bells is safe and always has been. Everyone here knew me, my parents, and my grandparents. It's like the whole town is my family. Especially when my parents moved to Florida, I was really glad for the community here. I never felt like I was on my own."

"That's beautiful."

She rolled her eyes. "Oh, come on. Admit it. You think I sound insane."

"It's not anything that's familiar to me, but no, I don't think you sound insane. It sounds nice."

She smiled at him, and Michael forgot about the hockey game for a while as he let himself get lost in her eyes. He'd tried not to come on too strong in the beginning, and then he was trying to figure out how she felt about him, but he wasn't trying to hide anything anymore.

"Okay, rapid fire questions," she said.

"What?"

"Don't think, just answer."

"Are you serious?"

"Yes. This is the fastest way for us to get to know each other."

He laughed. "Okay, now I think you sound insane."

"Are you going to humor me or not?"

"Fine, fine."

"Okay," she said. "Siblings?"

"None."

"Same," she said. "Your turn."

"Hobby?"

"Cooking."

Michael scoffed. "That's your job, not a hobby."

"My job is baking. Cooking is totally different."

"Fine."

"What's your hobby?"

"Reading."

"Ah, hence the interest in the bookstore. Okay, best Christmas gift you ever got?"

"A guitar. You?"

She smiled. "A piano. I guess we've both got a musical streak."

"I guess so. Favorite movie?"

"Christmas or regular?"

He laughed loudly. "Somehow, I think it'll be the same answer for you either way."

She smirked in a way that betrayed that he had caught her. "*It's a Wonderful Life*. You?"

"The entire *Indiana Jones* franchise."

"Ugh. That's such a stereotypical guy answer."

"What can I say? I like a good story."

"Is that a good story, though?"

Michael let out an overly dramatic gasp. "How dare you?"

They both laughed, and when the buzzer sounded to indicate the end of the first period, they both seemed a little surprised that they had missed almost the entire game so far. Though he loved a good hockey game, Michael couldn't have said that he felt sorry he'd missed out on this one so far.

The big screen on the far wall lit up as the arena started up a kiss cam. Michael had always thought that kiss cams were kind of weird because the kisses always looked so forced, and who really wanted to kiss on a jumbotron at a hockey game in front of thousands of people? But the kiss cam here felt different. Everyone in here knew each other, and it showed. People cheered for each other, even playfully heckled each other, and every kiss looked so genuine. There were young couples and elderly couples, and everyone looked so happy. Michael was pleasantly surprised to find that he recognized a few faces, too, meaning he'd finally spent enough time in Bells not to feel like an outsider.

What he hadn't expected was to see Emily's face on the screen, and he was so shocked that it took him a moment to realize that the confused guy to her right was, in fact, him. They exchanged a nervous look and laugh, but everyone around them cheered. Emily playfully waved her hand at the camera and kissed Michael on the cheek. The gesture was surprising, and yet, he felt as if it had been the most natural thing in the world for her to do. The crowd, however, was not satisfied and continued to cheer. To appease the crowd, Michael asked, "May I?" and when Emily nodded, he kissed her quickly but sweetly, careful not to exploit the moment, but he desperately wanted the kiss to last longer than it did. The camera moved on, but it took a moment for the flushed color to leave Emily's cheeks and even longer for Michael's heart to stop beating so fast.

"So, uh," Emily said with a smile, "should we keep going with rapid fire questions?"

He nodded. "Sure." Though he really would have preferred to kiss her again, he was happy to do anything that meant spending more time with her and getting to watch her smile and talk and laugh, enchanting him with every move.

His phone buzzed, and he checked it because he was waiting for a message from the realtor, but he was surprised to see an email from his former boss at Rothstein Investments. He hadn't heard anything from them since he had quit—not that he had expected to hear anything. He was pretty sure he'd burned that bridge when he walked out. It was more than likely a random file they couldn't find or a key that was misplaced or a forgotten detail of a case that they were hoping Michael had some knowledge of. He considered opening the email right then and there out of sheer curiosity, but Darren's team scored a goal right at that moment, and he decided that, whatever it was, it could wait until tomorrow.

21

Emily

"A little higher right there," Emily said, pointing to the left. She'd offered to help Michael hang the rest of his decorations at Something Worth Reading, and boy, did he need the help. He'd hardly put up anything.

"How's that?" he said over his shoulder from the ladder.

"Perfect," she said, and Michael nailed the hook in the wall and arranged the lights.

Emily couldn't help but think about the fact that just a couple of weeks ago, she would have scoffed at the idea of helping Michael—or anyone, really—with their Deck the Shops entry. Winning had been so important to her, and while it still was, she just had some different priorities now. More things—more people—mattered to her now.

That had started before the kiss at the hockey game, but that kiss had certainly exacerbated matters. She'd been telling herself for weeks that she wouldn't let him get too close, and when he did, she told herself they were just friendly, then friends. Now, they had distinctly left friend territory. They'd gone on a date. They had *kissed*. If she focused, she could still feel his lips on hers, still picture his smile when he asked if he could as the entire community of Bells cheered around them. She'd always thought jumbotron kiss cams were tacky, but nothing about that moment had been anything but magical.

Michael moved the ladder and started climbing it again. "Only one more to go," he said. "How about right here?"

"Move it over a little," she said. "So it fits squarely in that corner."

"Got it."

Everything about this was the opposite of what she'd told herself she wouldn't let happen. Michael still didn't live here, and there was no guarantee that he would. More than once in the last few days, she'd found herself wondering what would happen if she won Deck the Shops and he didn't. That was what she wanted, wasn't it? But what would happen if he didn't win? Like him, she wasn't positive that Naomi would sell to him if he didn't win, and she was less sure that he'd stay without the bookstore.

But she also knew that she needed to win to have a chance at being heard and respected by her grandparents. What would happen if he won instead? Would he stay? And would her grandfather then have license to dismiss every one of her ideas?

This was exactly why she'd originally made the decision to stay out of it, to think of Michael as a passing stranger who was nice but not here to stay. It was easier that way with fewer feelings to muddy the waters.

But when she thought about that kiss...

"Okay," Michael said as he dismounted the ladder. "What do you think?"

She shook her head, focusing on the Michael in front of her asking about Christmas lights and not the Michael who had kissed her in front of the entire town. It was getting impossible to separate the two. "It looks great."

"Thanks so much for your help. I was kind of a mess trying to set all of this up."

"I could tell."

He rolled his eyes and smirked. "Ha ha. Okay, I put together some books that I could potentially use for the book tasting. What do you think of these?"

When Michael had told her his idea of doing a book tasting for the Deck the Shops event, it had admittedly made her a little nervous. It was a really good idea, and the more she thought about it and the more she saw his plans, the more she thought that it was a better idea than hers. She'd tried to go classic bakery and have cookie and cupcake decorating because who doesn't love that, but Michael's idea was so creative. It was sure to be a hit, and with the coveted last slot, his event would be memorable. He had a really good chance of winning, and here she was helping him secure the victory.

She looked through the stack of books, but she noticed a trend. "These are all classics."

"Yes," Michael said. "Is that a problem?"

"Aren't you targeting this event toward kids?"

"Kids can love the classics. They're classics for a reason."

"Of course, but if you're trying to get a kid who hates reading to fall in love with a book, the classics maybe aren't the place to start." She plucked a few bestsellers off of the table behind her. "What about these?"

"But those are so popular."

She chuckled. "Do you have a problem with popular? You sound like an early 2000s hipster."

He laughed. "No, I just mean, aren't they popular because everyone has already read them?"

"The big readers have, yes, but the kids who don't read haven't. At best, they've maybe seen the movie."

"Ugh, the blasphemy."

"Look, I'm not saying get rid of the classics. I'm just saying mix in some of these others. The big readers might gravitate to the classics."

He shuffled the books she had given him into the stack. "Okay, fair enough."

"Are you only doing kids' books, or will you have a section for adults, too?"

"I have an adults section, but now I'm afraid to show you the books I picked for that one."

Once again, Emily snagged a few titles she knew were popular as well as a couple that she had read herself and loved. She tried to vary the genres a little, but she definitely had a bias in her own reading habits. "Try these."

He added them to another stack. "Pretty soon, this will be half the bookstore."

She shrugged. "Not the worst thing. Maybe you'll sell more that way."

"Did I tell you my idea for a big finale?"

"No. You're doing a big finale?"

"I figured why not, you know? Since my event is the last one, I might as well capitalize on that." He grabbed a copy of *The Night Before Christmas* and held it up.

"A classic."

"I hope you mean that in a positive way," he said with a smirk.

"I do. So, what's your plan?"

"I've got Santa coming to read it to the kids at the end." He pointed to the arm chairs that sat in the corner of a reading nook Naomi had set up. "It's a surprise. He'll sit there and read the book."

"That's a really cute idea."

"Thanks."

"So, who is Santa? You?"

He laughed. "Like I could pull that off. Plus, I thought it would look weird if I randomly disappeared and then Santa appeared. No, I hired someone."

"Who?"

He hesitated, leaning against the counter. "Someone in town."

She rolled her eyes. "I know everyone in town. The same guy plays Santa every year and—" Michael avoided eye contact, surely knowing the realization she'd made. "You hired my grandfather to be Santa for your event?"

Another hesitation. "Maybe."

Playfully, she smacked his arm. "Traitor!"

He held up his hands in surrender. "Hey, he's the traitor, not me."

"I can't believe you stole my grandfather."

"Hey, he offered. I didn't even know he played Santa. It was all his idea when I mentioned the Santa idea."

"Well, of course it was his idea. He loves playing Santa."

Somewhat abruptly, Michael took both of Emily's hands in his and smiled sweetly, the warmth of his hands warming her all over. "I promise I did not try to steal Frank, and I will take out the Santa idea if it bothers you."

She could hardly focus on anything other than her fingers laced with his. "No, it's a cute idea." In a mocking voice, she said, "I guess it's fine that Grandpa is a Benedict Arnold."

He pulled her into a hug. "Glad you don't hate me even though I crossed into enemy lines."

She scoffed, but it was largely muffled by her face pressed against his chest. When he released, she didn't make much of an effort to move away. Perhaps it had only been a few seconds, but that hug felt like home, like that was where she was always supposed to be.

They didn't kiss—hadn't kissed since the hockey game—and while it was logical that they probably shouldn't until they figured out what they were and what was happening between them, it was hard for Emily to ignore how much she was hoping he would kiss her.

He took a step back. "I'm going to try to find some other books for the adults. Would you mind taking a look at the graphics I made on my laptop? I want to make sure they look good before I print them, and graphic design is not exactly my specialty."

"Sure," she said, but she watched him walk away before she directed her attention to his computer. She liked watching him wander through the aisles of Something Worth Reading. He looked at home surrounded by books.

She scrolled through the designs he had open, and while she jotted down a few notes for some color or font tweaks, she honestly didn't think there was that much to alter. These looked good, and she could picture them in the windows of the bookstore and on the tables at the events.

They hadn't really discussed whether or not they'd attend each other's events, but she had been assuming that they would. Even though they'd started out as competition and still were in many ways, she was eager to see how his event turned out. She had been pleasantly surprised by how well Michael's ideas and personality seemed to fit in Bells. Even though she knew he'd only ever lived in Chicago, she had such a hard time picturing him there. He just didn't fit.

A notification chime dinged from his laptop, and while she hadn't intended to look at the email that popped up, it was human nature to glance at the notification. She was surprised to see that it came from someone named Ron at Rothstein Investments. She was pretty sure Rothstein was the name of the place he'd quit just before coming to Bells. Against her better judgment, she opened the email.

Michael,

Thank you so much for hearing me out about the job offer. I've attached the official offer letter and benefits package. I hope that after the holidays we can—

Emily clicked the email closed, unwilling to read any more. She shook her head, wondering how she could have deluded herself so quickly and so convincingly. This was exactly what she knew would happen long before she ever got to know Michael. Sure, she wasn't able to picture him in Chicago, but what did that matter? Michael clearly could, and that was always going to be in the way.

She wondered if Naomi had given him some kind of indication that she wouldn't sell to him. Maybe he'd gotten tired of Bells. He had made a comment at the hockey game about whether or not it bothered her that everyone was always watching her. She hadn't thought anything of it at the time, but maybe that had been a sign that he was starting to shut down, starting to miss the city life. Maybe he was starting to tire of Bells, of the people, of the bookstore. Of *her*.

She grabbed her coat off of the coat rack and shrugged it on, hastily wrapping her scarf around her neck. She felt so stupid. She'd told herself not to get too close, not to let herself believe that he wanted to stay. She had known how it would end: Michael would leave, and she would be heartbroken. It had been inevitable, and despite every bit of her mind screaming at her for weeks not to let him in, she'd done it, and now it was her heart that would suffer.

She heard his footsteps returning from the back of the store, and she knew that if she saw his face, she would have an even harder time walking out the door, so she grabbed her bag, spun on her heel, and pushed through the door of the bookstore, ignoring the noise of the chime clanging overhead.

22

Michael

At the sound of the chimes, Michael headed out of the storeroom expecting to see a customer, but when he turned the corner from the back room, he was surprised to find that the bookstore was empty. He quickly looked around some of the aisles trying to figure out where Emily had gone in such a hurry. He checked the desk, thinking maybe she had left him a note, but when he saw that there was an unread email from Ron in his inbox, he feared that she had gotten the wrong impression.

He grabbed his coat and ran out the door, spotting Emily just down the street. She'd set her bag down on a bench, but she seemed unsure of where she was headed.

"Emily," he called out as he jogged toward her, but she didn't immediately make eye contact. "What happened? Why did you leave?"

Finally, she did turn to face him, and she looked like she was on the verge of tears. "When were you going to tell me?"

"Tell you what?"

"That you're leaving. Going back to Chicago."

"Who said I'm going back to Chicago?"

She rolled her eyes. "I'm not stupid, Michael. I didn't mean to, but I saw the email from Rothstein on your laptop. That's your old company, right?"

"It is, but—"

"How long have you been talking to them again about a job?"

"Not long, I mean—that's not what's happening." Michael was aware that he was floundering and contradicting himself, but he didn't know how to explain. He'd answered Ron's email from the other day mostly to get him off his back, but Ron had insisted on sending over an offer letter despite his protests. Likely, he wanted to prove to management that he had put forth an honest effort in getting Michael back, but Michael wasn't exactly waiting to see what the offer was. He wasn't interested.

Emily folded her arms. "You've obviously been talking to them. For how long? When did this start?"

Michael didn't want to answer, but the stony look on her face made it clear that she was not going to give up on getting an answer. "Sunday. He emailed me Sunday night."

Her face noticeably fell. "While we were at the hockey game?"

"That email came out of the blue. I had no idea it was coming. I didn't even read it then. I didn't—don't care what he has to say."

"But you responded to it later." It was a question, but she stated it like an accusation.

Michael rubbed the side of his face. "To tell him I wasn't interested."

Emily raised her voice. "He sent you an offer letter. It doesn't seem like you're not interested."

Though he didn't want to admit it, there was a tiny glimmer of truth to what Emily was saying. He wasn't interested in the job, and he didn't want to go back to Chicago, but it was hard to ignore the pride and excitement he felt when he read that they'd fired Eric after only a couple of weeks. Apparently Eric had turned out to be a huge disappointment, and Michael was humored at the idea that Eric had gotten fired. Ron's email was full of apologies for making the wrong choice, and he had begged Michael to reconsider taking the promotion he had thought was in the bag just a few weeks ago. If that email had come in before he had gotten to Bells or even early on, he might have jumped on the offer, but aside from the validation that came from knowing he'd been the right choice for the job, the email had only reminded him of what he had hated about the job: poor management, lack of respect, and all-consuming work hours that produced late night emails that came through on the weekends and expected immediate answers. A part of him still hadn't let go of the security and illusion of success that this job offered—and though he hadn't seen the offer letter yet, he was certain it included a hefty raise and more benefits—but that job didn't bring him joy, never had, and if his time in Bells had taught him anything, it was that happiness and a stable career didn't have to be mutually exclusive.

Michael said, "I told him to send the offer letter so I could turn it down."

"That makes no sense," she said, the icy wind whipping her hair in front of her face.

"He wasn't going to let it go until I saw the offer. I'm going to turn it down."

"Are you? What if you don't win Deck the Shops, huh, and Naomi won't sell you the bookstore? Can you really confidently say that no matter what happens, you won't take the job?"

"Of course," he said, but even he heard the slight uncertainty in his voice. He didn't know how to tell her that it wasn't uncertainty about Bells or her or the decision but rather the fear of doing the opposite of everything his parents had ever taught him, the opposite of the person he'd been for his entire adult life.

She let her arms drop to her side, a small, sad smile tugging at her mouth. "I knew this would happen. That's the most frustrating part, you know? I knew you wouldn't stay here. No one ever does."

"Emily, that's not what I—"

"Don't bother. I was stupid to let myself fall for you. I knew that this was temporary and that you'd leave as soon as the holidays were over. Guys like you always do."

A little frustrated, Michael said, "What does that even mean? You're not listening. I want to stay in Bells. Everything I've been doing here for weeks is because I'm not going back to Chicago or to the way my life used to be. I don't want it anymore. I want this." He tried to step toward her, reach for her hands.

"You don't belong here, Michael," she said, taking a step back from him. "You never did. Just go back to Chicago where you belong and leave me alone."

She didn't give him a chance to respond, just turned on her heel and walked in the direction of the bakery. He desperately wanted to follow her—knew that he should follow her—but what more could he say? She didn't want to listen, and he didn't know how to make her hear him. There was nothing else to do, so he went back to the bookstore, and though it had been slow all morning with basically no customers, he was acutely aware of how empty the space was without Emily in it.

23

When she swept the floor only to find no trash, dirt, or sugar on the floor, Emily realized she had spent so many hours cleaning the bakery that there was nothing else left to clean. Over the last few days, any minute she'd had that wasn't spend baking or interacting with customers had been spent deep cleaning every surface and crevice of the bakery. It was the only thing that even partially took her mind off of Michael. Now that everything was clean and the entire case was filled with pastries, she woefully realized that she was out of distractions.

Tired and a little sore from the extra manual labor, she dropped into the corner booth. The bakery was empty, and she didn't expect another rush for a couple of hours when everyone got off of work. It was close enough to the holidays now that kids were getting out of school and a lot of businesses were shutting down for the next few days. She expected Sweet Treats to enter its annual pre-Christmas rush any day now. Typically, the bakery would be insanely busy during that gap as many people bought desserts they wouldn't have to bake to make seemingly endless Christmas to-do lists just a little shorter. Emily looked forward to that chaos.

She tried to shove some napkins into the already full dispenser, but she wasn't really focused on it. She'd known getting involved with Michael was a bad idea, but she'd done it anyway. For that reason, she felt justified in her decision to cut Michael off and avoid any kind of interaction with him. Still, she couldn't ignore how much she missed him. How could the absence of someone who had only recently entered her life hurt as much as it did? She'd lived her entire life without him, and yet, she now felt like her life was incomplete without him.

The door chimed, and she looked up, hoping to see a customer she could help, but it was her grandmother. She was surprised to see that her grandmother was not accompanied by her grandfather. They rarely went anywhere without the other. Church choir was pretty much the only activity her grandmother did alone.

"Hi, honey," she said, sitting in the chair across from her. "How are you doing?"

"Fine," Emily said absent-mindedly, still not looking up from the napkins.

"Are you okay? You've seemed a little down lately."

"I'm fine."

Her grandmother leaned across the table and looked at her over the top of her reading glasses. "I know when you're not being honest with me. Is this about that handsome friend of Darren Moore's?"

Emily couldn't help but chuckle a little. "Grandma."

"Well?"

She let out a heavy sigh that rattled in her chest. "I like him, Grandma."

Her grandmother smiled sweetly. "I know, honey. I think we could all see it."

"I really like him, and I let myself believe that he wanted to stay in Bells, but I was wrong. He's going to move back to Chicago."

"He said that?"

Emily shook her head. "Not really, but I saw the job offer letter from his old boss. He worked so hard for a promotion and got passed over, but now, they desperately want him back."

"But has he accepted that offer?"

"Does it matter?"

Her grandmother sat up a little straighter in her chair. "Renee Moore tells me that he doesn't want it."

"That's what he said, but I just don't believe it."

"Why not?"

She flung her arms up in exasperation. "Because guys like him never do."

"Guys like what?"

"Guys from big cities who want excitement and bustling city centers and advancement. Bells is always too small for them. They get bored of it way too quickly. Bored of the city, bored of the entire town. Bored of me," she said, though that was the part she was least willing to admit. "They never want to stay, no matter what they say in the beginning. They all leave, just like—"

"Like?" her grandmother said, but Emily was unwilling to finish the sentence. "Just like Noah?"

Emily nodded, feeling the sting of tears welling in her eyes, and she was determined not to cry today.

"Oh, honey, you can't compare two different men or put the burdens of one on the other. Every person is different. Noah wasn't bored with you, but this life isn't what he wanted, just like the life he has isn't what you wanted. You weren't compatible even though you cared about each other."

"But Michael—"

"You've looked happier in the last few weeks with Michael than you did with Noah in the years that you dated. And Michael seems genuinely happy in Bells, and Noah never did. He was always restless, itching to move on to the next thing. He certainly wouldn't have watched Christmas movies with your grandparents while wearing one of your grandfather's ugly sweaters."

Emily couldn't stop the laugh that came out of her, and with it, a few stubborn tears slipped down her cheek. "I can't believe he put up with that."

She took Emily's hands in hers across the table. "He didn't just put up with it. He really enjoyed it, and he did it for you. Everything he's done this week has been about that bookstore or you. He's willing to do whatever it takes to be with you and to stay in Bells."

"But how does he know he won't get tired of all of this someday?"

"I think you're looking at it all wrong. It sounds like he got tired of the life he had. He wants this new life."

Reluctantly, Emily had to admit to herself that her grandmother made sense. Still, she couldn't get the image of that offer letter out of her head, and as far as she knew, Michael still hadn't turned the job down. It was hard for her to trust that anything her grandmother was saying was true as long as she felt like he was keeping one foot in Chicago.

"Are you going to go to the event at Something Worth Reading?" her grandmother asked.

Emily shook her head. "I don't think I can. I don't want to see him again."

"I don't think that's true."

"I don't think I can *handle* seeing him again. Besides, I doubt he'll come to the Sweet Treats event."

"You both put a lot of effort into these events. I hope you'll change your mind and see what he came up with. You helped him so much with it. Promise me you'll think about it?"

"Fine, I'll think about it," Emily said, but she felt sure that she didn't want to go to his event. It would be easier on her in the long run if she never laid eyes on him again. She couldn't stand the idea of seeing him in that bookstore, happy, fitting in so naturally, knowing that come the first of the year, he'd be back in a suit in a corporate office, stiff, the way he'd been the first day that he had walked into Sweet Treats.

"Good," her grandmother said, patting her hands and standing up. "I'm looking forward to seeing what you came up with for Sweet Treats. I hope you know that no matter what, your grandfather and I are so proud of you. I wouldn't want anyone else running this bakery. Your grandfather and I started this business out of love, both for each other and for baking and building community. We love you more than anyone in the world, and that's what makes you perfect for taking this business to the next phase of its life. You're doing everything right just by being you."

"Thanks, Grandma."

Without further comment, her grandmother left the store, and Emily was alone again. It was more important than ever that she win Deck the Shops now. Though her grandmother's comments sounded as if she was willing to listen to her ideas, she knew her grandfather was a stubborn nut to crack, and she still had something to prove.

Besides, if she lost Deck the Shops to a guy that would only quit the bookstore and leave town, well, she wasn't sure she would be able to handle that disappointment.

24

Michael

After rereading it for at least the fifth time, Michael sent the reply email to Ron, turning down the Rothstein Investments job offer, and slumped over Darren and Renee's kitchen island. Turning down the offer hadn't been the hard part, but it was important to him that he do so with grace. He was still kind of annoyed at how they had passed him over, so when they came crawling back and begged him to return, it was tempting to lash out or say something snide. Michael refused to be that kind of person. He'd turn down the job all right, and he knew that would leave them floundering, but that wasn't his responsibility anymore; it was Ron's and it was Eric's, and they had both failed.

Still, even though he knew he absolutely did not want that job back, it was a little scary to turn it down. He'd invested ten years into that company, into that job, and what had it gotten him? His plan was still to buy Something Worth Reading, but that wasn't a given at this point. He didn't know if he could win Deck the Shops, and he was less certain of his chances with Naomi. He didn't want to go back to Rothstein, but what would he do if he couldn't get the bookstore? It didn't feel like he could just look for another job in finance. His job at Rothstein had drained him, but he felt certain that it wouldn't be just Rothstein that would have that effect. He didn't want to go back to that world at all. He would start a business or buy a different one or get a job he would actually like.

But if not for Something Worth Reading, would any of that be in Bells?

The problem was that he hadn't just fallen for Emily. He had fallen for all of Bells. He loved the people here, he liked being close to Darren again, and he knew that he didn't want to be anywhere else. He just didn't know how to convince Emily to believe that he wanted to stay.

"Hey," Darren said as he and Renee walked through the front door. They had left to drop the boys off at a Christmas party. "We thought you'd be at the bookstore."

"I'm going in later today," he said. "I already have everything set up, so there really isn't much else to do. Naomi is working this morning."

Darren poured a cup of coffee from the pot Michael had just brewed and leaned against the counter opposite him. "What's going on, man? You've been in a funk for a couple of days."

"Is it Emily?" Renee asked, and when Michael furrowed his eyebrows, she added, "she told me what happened." She filled Darren in on the details.

"She won't even talk to me," Michael said. "I've tried calling and texting, but she ignores all of it. She's convinced that I'm moving back to Chicago, and it's like she doesn't hear me when I say that I don't want to go back."

"She's been burned before," Renee said. "It's just hard for her to believe you, I think. That's not a reflection of you, but she has a hard time trusting."

"I just don't know how to fix it."

"Well, you better figure it out," Darren said. "I've known you a long time, and I've never seen you look at anyone the way you look at her."

Michael shrugged somewhat sheepishly. "You know, I just came here to see you. I thought I would take a break, let the hurt feelings fade, hang out with you, then move back to Chicago. I had even researched job openings and updated my resume when I first got here. But first I met Emily, and then the bookstore thing just kind of happened, and, I don't know, all of a sudden, I'm doing everything I can to stay in a town I never thought I'd even visit a month ago."

"Okay," Darren said, "how serious are you about moving here? I know you've mentioned it, but level with me."

"I turned down the offer from Rothstein this morning, and I talked to the realtor you recommended. Shayna?" Michael said to Renee, and she nodded. "Shayna found a couple of properties that would all be perfect to rent, and they're all available in January. There's one I really like just outside of downtown with a lake behind it. It's pretty much just a matter of signing the papers."

"What about the bookstore?" Darren asked.

Michael rubbed the sides of his face. "I have no idea what's happening with that. I'm not sure I will know until after Deck the Shops is over. But I really hope I'm able to convince Naomi."

Michael was afraid to admit to Darren and Renee, much less himself, how much he wanted the bookstore. He'd never been excited to go to work every day until now, and it seemed like every day he came up with another idea that he wanted to implement. It was laughable, really, that he ever thought he could do anything with his life that didn't involve books. He knew why it had taken him so long to figure it out, but he still wished he hadn't wasted so much of his life on a dead-end job that had only brought him stress. He wanted the bookstore so much that he had seriously considered how he would try to sway Naomi if he didn't win Deck the Shops.

He continued, "But it's hard to think about seeing Emily every day and not being with her."

"Why don't you go over to the bakery and try to talk in person? We're out of cookies anyway."

Michael snorted. "I don't want to ambush her if she doesn't want to talk to me. Besides, she's busy. Her Deck the Shops event is tomorrow, and I don't want to get in her way."

"Can I say something?" Renee asked, and Michael nodded. "I think maybe you do need to get in the way. Emily is one of my closest friends, but sometimes, she gets too in her head about things, and she has a hard time getting out of her own way. I think she needs to see how serious you are about her and Bells."

Darren asked, "Are you going to the Sweet Treats event?"

"Well, I didn't think I would after the fight, but you think I should?"

Renee nodded. "Definitely. You helped her so much with that. You should be there. She wants you there."

He sat up a little straighter. "Did she say that?"

"No, but I know her. You miss her, and she misses you. Trust me. Her night won't feel right without you there."

"Then I'll go. I really didn't want to miss out. I'm excited to see what she landed on for the dessert flights."

Darren patted his stomach. "You and me both."

Michael stood up, downing the last of his coffee and grabbing his coat. He was invigorated and motivated to do whatever it would take to stay in Bells. "I'm going to win her back," he said.

"I have no doubt," Darren said.

"I know she makes you happy," Renee said, "but you make her happy, too."

"Honestly, I didn't know I could feel as good as I have these past few weeks. I'm going to stay in Bells, whatever it takes. I'm going to the bookstore. I have to finish up some things."

He quickly put on his coat and waved to Darren and Renee as he walked out of the house. He was going to win Emily back, convince Naomi to sell the bookstore, and put a deposit down on the rental property with the lake. He wouldn't have believed it just a month ago, but he was done with Chicago, done with jobs he hated, done with living a lonely life. Bells was his home now, and he was going to stay.

25

Emily

Plugging in the last strand of lights, Emily stepped back and marveled at her handiwork. She had fully committed to the winter wonderland theme with blue and white lights and snowflakes everywhere, and she was really happy with how it had turned out. Sweet Treats definitely had more lights than just about any other business in town, but honestly, that felt right. Her grandparents had brought so much light into Bells and even into her own life, and it felt appropriate that she reflect that in the shop.

The timer in the kitchen went off, so she started plating the cookies she had pulled out of the oven earlier. She had prepped a lot of the baked goods yesterday so that they would be cool and ready to frost and decorate, but she had wanted to have at least a few fresh out of the oven for the delicious smell—hopefully, it would encourage people to decorate and buy more cookies.

There was a knock at the door, and though the event didn't start for a few more minutes, she saw Bella and Mia outside of the door, so she let them in.

"I brought the boxes," Bella said, holding up a large paper bag.

With an exhale of relief, Emily said, "Oh, thank you so much. I can't believe I forgot to pick those up before the store closed." Emily had ordered little to-go boxes for everyone to put their cookies and cupcakes in after decorating, but in all of the chaos, she hadn't gotten them. Without them, people would have to carry their desserts, and that didn't bode well for sales.

"It looks so good in here," Mia said as she hung her coat on the coat rack. "It's like a winter wonderland."

"That's exactly what I was going for," Emily said.

"I love it," Mia said. "It's so pretty. It really looks like you because it's so over the top in a good way, but it doesn't feel overwhelming or chaotic."

Emily smiled, but there was a pang in her heart. She owed that to Michael. Without him, she certainly would have gone overboard, and nothing would have matched. It definitely would have been overwhelming, and she didn't need to cause sensory overload in her customers when they should be having fun at a Christmas event.

"What is it?" Bella asked. Emily tried to snap out of it, but she struggled to hide her watering eyes, her counterfeit smile. "Come on, talk to us."

Emily sat down at one of the tables, and Bella and Mia each took a chair as well. "It's Michael," she said, trying to keep her voice from shaking. "The theme was his idea. Originally, I had way more decorations, but I didn't have a theme, and he encouraged me to centralize what I was doing."

Mia took Emily's hand in hers and smiled. "It was a good idea."

Emily nodded. "Yeah, it was. I'm sorry, this is so stupid. I shouldn't be crying over decorations. It's not that serious."

Bella said, "We all know it's not really about the decorations."

"He just got me, you know?" Emily said with a sniffle. "So many people would have just told me to do less, not to try so hard, but not Michael. He helped me make my own idea better, not change my idea entirely."

"He helped you be the best version of yourself," Bella said.

Emily nodded. "Exactly."

"Have you talked to him?"

"No, not since the other day when I blew up at him over the job offer. I totally overreacted."

"Then make it right," Mia said, handing Emily a napkin. "Talk to him."

"It's pointless," Emily said, dabbing her eyes. "I don't think he wants to talk to me, and what would I even say? Either he took the job and there's no point or he didn't and really wants to stay and I'm the jerk who broke his heart anyway."

"I think you're underestimating him," Bella said. "From every interaction I've had with him, he seems like a really nice guy. Maybe you should just give him a chance."

Emily nodded, but she stood up abruptly and dabbed her eyes again. "It doesn't matter right now. Tonight is my Deck the Shops event, and I'm not going to lose focus. I want tonight to be flawless."

"Well, it looks like you're off to a great start."

"Can we do anything to help you finish setting up?" Mia asked.

"Just lay out the boxes on this table here. I have to finish putting out the cookies."

***

It was only about halfway through the event, but everything was going perfectly. There had been a steady stream of people eager to decorate some Christmas pastries, so much so that Emily had struggled a little bit to find seats for everyone and keep up with the demand for more cupcakes and cookies. She was glad she had taken the risk and baked an extra batch of each this morning—they were definitely going to use them.

Most importantly, the flights had been hugely popular. Everyone had complimented the variety but still felt like the traditional holiday flavors they were used to were honored. Emily's idea had been good, but she had needed to refine it. Sometimes she was so much of a dreamer that she didn't always execute well or even think about how to execute it. Michael had helped her see that.

Her grandparents had offered to help her, but it was important to her that she do this on her own. She wanted to prove that she could and also give her grandparents a chance to sit back and enjoy. Mia and Bella had jumped in a few times to help, but otherwise, she was handling it, and everything was working.

After she got the next group settled and decorating, her grandmother pulled her to the side.

"This whole evening is lovely," Grandma said. "I'm very impressed with what you've done tonight."

"Thank you."

"I really like the cookie and cupcake decorating. It's so fun and festive. That's the heart of Deck the Shops: family holiday events."

"That was the goal." Emily smiled, but she had always known that her grandfather was the one she really had to convince. Her grandmother was so sweet and generally proud of her, and she knew that she would support whatever she did. It was her grandfather who held the reins a little tighter and resisted change. He hadn't said much to her tonight, and Emily wondered if he was avoiding her. He looked happy, and he was interacting with all of the kids, but she couldn't help but feel like he either hated the idea or didn't want to admit that he liked it. She wasn't sure which would be worse.

"Are you sure I can't help you?" Grandma asked.

Emily was about to shoo her away sweetly, encouraging her to relax, but she was distracted by the door chime jingling. She looked up to see how many people were coming in so that she could decide where to seat them and what supplies to grab, but she was stopped in her tracks by the sight of Darren and Renee and, most importantly, Michael following behind them.

She'd been convinced that Michael absolutely would not show up tonight. She'd given him every reason to stay away, and she knew that she had already counted herself out of his Deck the Shops event, so it seemed like the obvious conclusion that he wouldn't attend hers. She wondered if maybe Darren and Renee had dragged him here or if he came because he had nothing else to do. She wondered if it would be possible to avoid him the entire time he was in her bakery.

The problem was that she realized that the entire time she was entertaining a million "what-ifs" that she had been staring at him, unwillingly lost in the golden flecks sparkling in his brown eyes. He smiled and waved, but thankfully before she had to decide how she would react to him, he got pulled in a different direction by a group of people. It looked like he had gotten friendly with Luke and his wife Shayna, and she wondered how they crossed paths. She knew that Renee and Shayna were old friends from high school, so maybe Darren and Renee had gotten together with them and Michael had just happened to be there.

What was surprising wasn't that he had met some of Darren and Renee's friends; it was surprising to see how well he fit in with them. An outside observer would probably think that he was from Bells, that these were long-time friends. She'd noticed it before, and it was still true now: Michael fit in with Bells and everyone in it.

Unfortunately, she was still staring at him, so when he glanced in her direction, the slight jerk of his head betrayed surprise. Emily forced a smile again, and Michael pulled himself from conversation with Luke and Darren and walked toward her. She had spent so much time assuming that Michael wouldn't come to Sweet Treats tonight and talking herself up for tonight that she hadn't considered what she would do if he did show up. She knew Michael was too kind to cause a scene, but what would a conversation between them look like at this point?

"Hey," he said once he was close enough. "The place looks great. I love all of the blue lights."

She shrugged. "It was your idea."

He nodded, fidgeting a little with the cuff on his sleeve. "I hope it's all right that I came tonight. I really wanted to see your Deck the Shops event in its final form."

"Of course it's okay. Thanks for coming." Emily hated how forced and civil that sounded, but she didn't know how to make it sound any other way.

"How's it going so far?"

"Really well. It's been this crowded pretty much all night."

He smiled, but it looked so much more genuine than anything she felt like she had said that had all sounded so false to her. She simultaneously hated and loved how kind his face still looked. It would have been easier to avoid letting him back in if he were angry, but she also knew that she would have been crushed if he had shut her out. She couldn't deny that the way he smiled at her still made her feel warm, and despite everything, she wanted to enjoy that feeling.

He lowered his voice slightly and asked, "Any verdict from your grandparents yet?"

"My grandmother is really enjoying it, but I haven't had a chance to talk to Grandpa yet. I have no idea what he's thinking."

"Well, it all looks fantastic. I think I'll have to decorate some cupcakes, if that's all right. I haven't come by in a while, and the Moore house is woefully low on desserts."

Emily couldn't help but laugh. She gestured to an open seat and said, "Be my guest."

He started in that direction, but he hesitated when he was so close to her that she could smell his cologne, a rich scent reminiscent of firewood. "By the way, I wanted to tell you that I turned down the offer from Rothstein.

I was always going to turn it down. I guess—I guess I just wanted to know that they knew they were wrong. Maybe that's prideful of me, but I liked knowing that they still wanted me."

"Of course. It makes sense."

"And I talked to a realtor—Shayna over there. She showed me some places that are available to rent starting in January. I just wanted you to know that I was serious when I said I want to stay in Bells. This town, the bookstore, Darren and Renee, your grandparents." He paused. "You. All of this here is everything I ever wanted. If I don't win Deck the Shops and get Something Worth Reading, I'll figure it out. But I don't want to be anywhere else. If I lose Deck the Shops, then I lose, but at least I'll know that you won. I'm staying, Emily. I know I've only been here a short time, but Bells is home. It's felt like home since the day I walked into Sweet Treats and you conned me into buying way too many desserts."

A laugh burst from her lips. "I also gave you a free pie, to be fair."

He smiled sweetly. "I don't suppose you have any chocolate cream pies to decorate?"

She shook her head. "Sorry, fresh out."

"I guess I'll just have to wait for them, then."

And with that, he joined Darren, Luke, and Shayna at a table and started decorating a cupcake, and Emily was left with his words ringing in my ears. She had thought that she had sabotaged any chance that she and Michael had, but he had made it clear that he was still leaving the door open for them. She had also thought that she wanted to sabotage it, that it would be easier than the pain she'd feel when he left. But Michael's leaving was not a "when" but an "if." Not even that.

Renee walked up to her, seeing her blinking tears from her eyes, and touched her arm gently. "Are you okay?"

"Did you bring Michael tonight?"

"I mean, we drove him, but he really wanted to come. He wanted to make things right with you," she said, and Emily nodded. "What did he say?"

Emily relayed everything to Renee, still just as shocked by the words as she said them as she had been when he had said them. "I just thought there was no chance, you know? I thought he didn't want to be here or that I had ruined any chance we had, but he seems really serious."

"He is serious. All he has talked about for weeks is the bookstore, Shayna's properties, and you."

"But what if he loses Deck the Shops?"

"It's no secret that he wants to win, and I think he'll be disappointed if he loses, but I think he wants to stay no matter what."

"That's what he said, but it's hard to know until the contest actually ends."

Renee put a hand on each of Emily's arms. "Emily, I think at some point, you're going to have to let go of Noah. Every guy is not him. Michael is certainly not him. You've been happier with him in the last few weeks than you were in your entire relationship with Noah. He didn't want to be here, but Michael does. I think you have to let him in."

She nodded, but it was still hard to believe. "What if I win, and he doesn't get the bookstore? What if I lose, losing something important to me?"

She gestured in the direction of my grandparents. "Look how happy they are. I don't think you're disappointing them regardless of what happens with Deck the Shops. I think you need to trust them, too. Do you believe in your ideas for the bakery?"

"Yes."

"Do you want to be with Michael?"

Emily nodded. "Yes, I think so."

"Then go for what you want. Stop holding yourself back."

She wanted to believe Renee—really, she did—but she just didn't know how to relax, how to trust that everything would work out. "How do I even do that?"

"Go to the Deck the Shops event at Something Worth Reading."

After giving Emily's arm a squeeze, Renee joined Darren and the others at the table, and Emily was left to consider her words. She had sworn off of going to Michael's Deck the Shops event, but she had also assumed he would never show up at her event, and he had. How did that change things? Was she willing to take the risk and show up?

Renee's words were ringing in her ears, and even if she didn't quite want to admit it, Emily knew she was right. Eventually, she would have to let go of her fear and take a leap of faith.

26

Michael

"You have ten minutes to flip through the book in front of you," Michael said, pointing to the Christmas themed stopwatch he'd pulled up on his laptop. Before now, he hadn't even known that Christmas themed stopwatches were something that existed, but he had learned a lot in his time in Bells. "When the timer plays 'Jingle Bells,' that's your signal to rotate clockwise. Is everyone ready?" The kids cheered. "Ready, set, go!"

The kids tore open the books and started reading, sometimes chatting with those around them. Michael had decided to start with just the kids so that they could get their part of the book tasting done early. He figured that would mean that while they were listening to Santa—read: Emily's grandfather Frank—the adults were free to do their own book tasting while the kids were entertained.

He was pleasantly surprised by how many kids had shown up. He still really didn't have a sense of how involved the kids in Bells would be in an event like this, and while he was aware that the main draw was the adver-tised "special surprise," he was still enthused by the turnout. Sometimes it seemed like getting kids to be excited about reading was a losing game, but tonight proved that that didn't have to be true. If nothing else, he was proud of that.

"This is such a cute idea," one of the moms said to him. "My son loves to read, but he reads so fast that I can't keep up, and I don't know anything about books for his age group."

"I'm glad you like it," Michael said. "Hopefully he can find something he likes that he hasn't read yet."

"I've got the opposite problem," another mom said. "My son won't ever read, but he was willing to give this a shot." She pointed at the little blonde boy who was poring over a *Percy Jackson* book. "He actually looks pretty interested in that one."

"Oh, everyone loves that series," the first mom said. "My son has the whole series, actually. You could borrow them if you like."

"Thanks," she said, but she smiled at Michael, "but I think I'll buy them as a Christmas present. I'd love to support the bookstore."

"Thanks so much," Michael said. "But I should warn you that that series is long. I think you should know how many books you're signing up to buy."

She laughed. "That's nice of you, but if it gets Sam to read, I'll buy anything."

"I'll set aside the box set at the register for you then."

The timer went off, so he reset it and prompted the kids to rotate. Some were actually a little disappointed to leave a book they had found interesting, and others were excited to see something new, and honestly, Michael considered both of those reactions a win. He plucked the *Percy Jackson* box set off of the shelf—Naomi had at least five complete copies of that series since it was so popular—and tucked it behind the register. He spotted Frank walking through the door with a somewhat suspicious looking bag, so he gestured for him to walk to the back while the kids were distracted.

He opened the door to the storeroom, and Frank walked in. "You can change in here. I'll call you out when it's time. The kids still have a few rotations left, so you've got time."

"Sounds good," Frank said, taking off his coat and scarf.

"Thanks again for doing this."

Frank laughed and slapped him on the back. "It's not a favor. You're paying."

Michael smiled. "Still. I appreciate it."

The unsaid words were that Michael was glad Frank was still willing to do this despite Michael and Emily's falling out. He wasn't sure how much Frank knew, and he definitely didn't think Frank was petty enough to go back on his word, but he still worried about it. He hoped that the fact that he and Frank were still friendly and that he had had a chance to talk to Emily at Sweet Treats the other night were signs that there was still hope for them. He certainly hoped that there was.

He left Frank to get ready and reset the timer for the next round. It was going well—the kids were really getting into it now, and several had abandoned their rounds to beg their parents for certain books, and all of the parents coyly deflected with some kind of "Maybe you should ask Santa for it" response, and once their kids walked away, asked Michael to put them on hold for them. In a short amount of time, he had at least twenty-five books lined up to be purchased the next day away from little prying eyes. This was better than he expected, and he was mostly glad to see kids as excited about reading as he was as a child.

Right after a rotation, he spotted Naomi slip in the back. She'd told him that she would be late, and he had actually been glad for it. It meant that she would come in once the event was already rolling, and she had walked in at the perfect time. The kids weren't even really staying in their seats at this point because they were having so much fun.

Naomi made no effort to move toward him, so he walked over to her. "They look like they're enjoying themselves," she said when he got close.

He nodded and held out a sheet of paper. "And this is the list of parents who have already put books on hold to purchase."

She raised her eyebrows but otherwise betrayed no sign of emotion or opinion. "When are the adults doing their round?"

"Once the kids finish. I have a surprise for them."

"What is it?"

His smile was mischievous. "I can't ruin the surprise for you, now can I?"

Naomi looked a little surprised that he was holding out on her. It was a risk not to tell her, but she was the one who had told him to treat the bookstore as if it was his own. Through her surprise, he saw the edges of her mouth curl into a smile that matched his own.

"Well," she said, "I'm glad to see the kids having fun with books."

Michael stared wistfully at the kids. "You know, Christmases for me as a child weren't very magical—honestly, nothing about my childhood was magical, just ordinary—but the brightest spot of my childhood is the bookstore my parents would take me to after school and in the summers. It was smaller than this one, but I thought it was just pure magic. How else do you describe a place that lets you travel to new places, live other lives, all without leaving the room? I just always thought that that bookstore was the happiest place in the world to be. I'm glad to see that kids haven't given up on that kind of magic."

When Naomi didn't say anything, he shifted his gaze to her, and he found that she was staring at him, not an inch of her expression readable. She could have equally been thinking he was right or that he was crazy, and he would have no idea. After a moment, she simply nodded and said, "I'm going to walk around a little. Looks like the kids are almost done."

She did as she said, and Michael saw that the last timer was running out. Hopefully Frank was ready to go. The timer went off, and Michael said, "That's it! Thanks for playing my game. Did you have fun?"

The kids all screamed, "Yes!"

"I'm so glad. Well, I have one more surprise for you, but do you still have enough energy for it?" The kids screamed even louder. "Okay, I need everyone to come sit on this carpet."

The kids immediately ran over to the colorful rug under the armchair that was tucked in the corner. They had to squish together to all fit, but they eagerly did so, staring up at Michael in anticipation.

Michael clapped his hands and said, "Okay, raise your hand if you saw a book you really liked." Almost every kid raised their hand. "Well, it's really close to Christmas, did you know that? I think you might able to get the book you wanted for Christmas this year, but you'll have to ask someone very special, someone who has the magic to get it to you overnight. Do you know who that is?"

Surprisingly, one kid immediately yelled, "Amazon!"

All of the adults in the room erupted into laughter. Well, Michael thought, he isn't totally wrong. "I was thinking of someone even more magical."

Several kids yelled, "Santa!"

"That's right! Santa, could you come out here?"

The moment that the storeroom door opened, the kids exploded into screams of excitement. Frank played the part very well, and it was obvious to Michael why he always played Santa around town. He was so convincing as Santa that even Michael found himself caught up in the bit.

Frank sat down on the chair, and once the kids quieted down, Michael said, "Now, Santa wants to hear all about the books you want for Christmas, but first, he wants to read you his favorite book. How does that sound?"

The kids cheered, and Michael handed Frank *The Night Before Christmas.* Once he started reading, Michael gathered the adults around the tables for their book tasting. He explained the process, set a quieter timer for them that wouldn't disturb the kids, and they started reading. He had set up different genres on different tables and tried to mix in classics with more modern books in each genre.

He had Emily to thank for that. The list of books he had put out was so much more diverse and complete because of her. He couldn't help but feel like that was what Emily had done for him in his life: she had made it more complete. Michael hadn't known what he had been missing in his life because he'd never really had it to begin with. But Emily, her family, Bells—all of it was everything he didn't know he wanted. He didn't expect her to come tonight, but that didn't change how much he had hoped that she would. Tonight wouldn't have become what it had without her, and even though he had put a lot of work into planning the event, it felt incomplete without her.

As if summoned, Emily walked through the door, accompanied by Darren and Renee. Pretty much immediately, Darren joined the mystery/thriller table, and Renee joined the romance table, but Emily walked toward him. She looked beautiful in the long red coat she was wearing—a coat she noticeably did not take off, implying she wasn't staying long—her hair tousled by the wind outside. The entire room felt different the moment that she walked in.

"Mind if I drop in?" Emily said.

Michael smiled wide. "I never mind. I'm really glad you came."

She shrugged, seemingly in an attempt to look casual. "I wanted to see how it all turned out. It looks like it's going really well." She glanced over at Frank. "Plus, I never get tired of seeing Grandpa as Santa."

"He's very good at it. I'm impressed."

She fidgeted with the hem of her sleeve. "You know, I dated this guy Noah a while back. He was a nice guy, but he just didn't want to be in Bells. He liked big cities not small towns, and he found Bells really suffocating. We tried to make it work, and he really tried to be comfortable here, but we just hurt each other in the long run. It was never going to work out." She paused a moment, then continued. "The problem I've always run into with people who aren't from here is that they view Bells as a stepping stone, not a final destination. They like to make comments that a place like Bells is nice as a kid, but eventually, you have to grow out of it. I just don't agree. This right here is all I've ever wanted. I never wanted anything other than to run Sweet Treats, raise a family around my family, and—well, and watch Grandpa play Santa. Does that really make my goals less than? Am I aiming too low?"

"I don't think so."

She smiled. "I don't think so either. I'm happy here, and I don't expect everyone in the world to want the same thing I do, but I don't want to pretend that I should want something different. Bells is home. It always will be."

"I had never seen a place like Bells before these last few weeks. I didn't even know to think of something like this as what I wanted, but as soon as I saw it, there was no contest. I never want to be anywhere again."

"Won't you miss Chicago?"

He shrugged. "There are things I like about it, sure, but when I think about what made me happy about Chicago, it was the bookstore I visited as a child, hockey games, and college with Darren. I can have all of that here."

She tilted her head in the direction of Naomi who was watching Frank read to the kids. "Has she given you any indication of what she's thinking?"

"None. How about your grandparents?"

"Not really. I mean, my grandma told me she really liked everything, but she didn't say much else, and my grandpa hasn't said anything at all."

He leaned in toward Emily. "So I guess we still don't know what's going to happen."

"I guess not. But I wanted to tell you that your help with Sweet Treats made a big difference. I don't think I would have had the success that I did without you."

"I was thinking the same thing about you before you walked in here. I know we both want to win, but I want you to know that if I don't, I don't regret anything. This whole thing helped me decide what I really want in life. Thank you for that."

She smiled again, and it seemed genuine. "You're welcome. I have to duck out, but maybe I'll see you at the Christmas festival tomorrow?"

Michael couldn't help but laugh. "How many Christmas festivals does Bells do?"

"This is the last one, I promise. It's where they announce the winner of Deck the Shops."

"Then I'll see you there."

Michael watched Emily leave, mostly because he just couldn't look away, and though he still wasn't totally sure where they stood, he knew that he was going to see her tomorrow, and that was all he needed to have hope in them.

27

Emily

Sweet Treats had been busy all morning. Christmas was only two days away, and the last minute rush that always happened seemed to be in overdrive. Emily hadn't stopped running around for hours. Finally, there was a lull. Because everyone was running last minute errands, there weren't really many people just sitting in the bakery eating, so it was pretty quiet. She sat at the counter to fill out some inventory reports, but she was interrupted when her grandparents came in.

"Hey," she said. "I thought you weren't coming in until after Christmas."

"We weren't, but we know you're working some long hours this week, so we wanted to stop by to see you. Can we talk?"

Emily didn't know if that was good or bad, but it didn't really matter. She relocated to a table, and her grandparents sat across from her.

"We wanted to talk about Deck the Shops," her grandpa said.

Her grandma added, "Specifically, we wanted to make sure we were being clear." That sounded somewhat ominous, but Emily decided it was best not to say anything and let them continue. "We want you to know that we were both really impressed with what you put together for Deck the Shops. The cookie and cupcake decorating was a wonderful idea, and

I think everyone really enjoyed it. But my favorite part was the drink and dessert flights. Those were so charming and unique."

Emily sat up a little straighter. That was the idea she was most proud of, but it was also the biggest risk. She really didn't know how those ideas would land with her grandparents, but they had been very popular at the event. She imagined that if Sweet Treats sold them, they would have made a killing.

Her grandpa leaned forward. "I think that maybe I was a little hasty in rejecting the idea of serving drinks. I just never wanted to bother with it, but drinks are definitely a money maker, and you do them so well."

"Thank you. Really, that means a lot."

He took his wife's hand in his. "I guess—well, I guess I was afraid that if you could run this without us, that we were obsolete, and that if your ideas were better than ours, then maybe we had become outdated. What we realized is that we were evaluating your ideas through our own eyes, our skills, and our limitations. We didn't feel like we were equipped to do some of those new ideas, but we didn't think about your skill set. You're so much better at this than we ever were."

"Oh, that's not true," Emily said. "I can't even believe everything you've done to build Sweet Treats. All of my ideas and my effort have been an attempt to live up to your legacy, not change it."

"We see that," Grandma said. "But you're capable of taking Sweet Treats to the next level, and that's what it needs. You're already doing it. We just needed to trust you. It's okay that you're better at this than us because we're so proud of who you are."

Her grandfather continued, "I know our deal originally was that if you won Deck the Shops that we would consider your ideas, but that deal is pointless. We don't need Sweet Treats to win to see that you were right about all of your ideas. We had more customers in here that night than we ever have at a Deck the Shops event. You know what you're doing. We just need to trust you."

Emily felt tears welling in her eyes. "Really?"

Her grandmother nodded. "We're going to keep stepping back slowly from the company, let you take the reins a little more. We'll always be here to support and help you, but Sweet Treats is yours now."

"And," Grandpa said, a wry smile spreading under an eye roll, "I might even reconsider my stance on cupcakes."

"You're kidding," Emily said, laughing.

"On one condition: do you have any more of those apple cider cupcakes you made? They were delicious."

"I do. I'll go get them right now." They all stood, but before Emily walked away, she threw her arms around them in an embrace. "Thank you so much. All I wanted was for you to believe in me."

"We always did," Grandma said. "We just didn't always show it well."

"I'll go get those cupcakes."

Emily practically skipped into the kitchen, ecstatic at the news. She'd thought that winning Deck the Shops was the most important thing to her, but it really wasn't. It was just symbolic of what she truly wanted: her grandparents' approval. They had done so much for her in her life, and she was in such awe of all that they had accomplished and everything that they were. In some ways, it was a tremendous amount of pressure to live up to them, but maybe that was the problem. She was never going to be exactly like them, and that was okay. She needed to be herself.

Winning Deck the Shops didn't really matter anymore—she'd already won the prize she wanted. But as she boxed up a few cupcakes for her grandfather, Michael crossed her mind. She didn't need to win Deck the Shops anymore, but what if she did? What if she won and Michael lost? Her winning might mean that Naomi wouldn't sell the bookstore to Michael, and she knew how important that was to him. Suddenly, she found herself desperately hoping for a different outcome to Deck the Shops than she had in weeks.

28

Michael

It had taken a while for Michael to clean the bookstore after the Deck the Shops event last night, but it was finally looking normal aside from the Christmas decorations he had left up. It hadn't been super busy today, but many of the parents who had put books on hold had already come to pick them up. He was basically just waiting on the last few to come in.

For maybe the first time in his life, Michael was proud of what he had done. When he had graduated college and then graduate school, he had felt proud of his hard work, and when he landed the job at Rothstein, he was proud of himself. He had done work at Rothstein that he knew was high quality. But this was a different kind of pride that he had never experienced before. He was impressed by what he accomplished, sure, but none of that other work had ever been meaningful. He had never felt like anything he had done had really mattered until now. He had inspired people, kids and adults alike, to love reading, to take a risk on a new story, to support an indie bookstore. That felt so worthwhile.

The door chime jingled, and he expected to see another parent coming to pick up a book, but instead, he saw Naomi.

"Hey," he said. "What brings you here today?"

Naomi sat at one of the tables that was still out from the book tasting and gestured for Michael to join her, so he did. "I came to see you. The bookstore is closed tomorrow since it's Christmas Eve, and I probably won't be here again until the new year. I'm going to visit some family on the twenty-sixth. I wanted to talk about Deck the Shops."

Michael sat up a little straighter. He hadn't really expected to have this conversation until tonight after the winner was announced. He couldn't decide if it was a good sign or a bad one that she wanted to talk now before she knew if he had won.

"How do you feel about the event?"

"I feel great," Michael said, and though he was nervous, it was truthful. "I think it went really well."

"Why do you think it went well?"

"I mean, we've sold a ton of books today, but that's not really it. It just felt—I don't really know how to describe it."

"Try."

Michael thought for a moment. "I've worked hard all my life, and I think I'm a really good employee, but that's all I've ever been: a nameless, faceless employee. But last night, and the whole time I've been working here, I've felt like I had meaning. I got to know you and everyone else in Bells. I got to know families. I mean, I've had people coming in all day to buy books as presents, and that's not exciting because it's income. It's exciting because people are excited about reading. My career has always been work and nothing else, but working here is working toward a goal that feels like it matters." Naomi nodded but didn't say anything. "I don't know if that made sense."

"It did. Here's another question. Did you only do this to win? In other words, if you don't win Deck the Shops tonight, will you feel it was worth-less?"

"I'll be disappointed if I don't win, but no, it wasn't worthless. I'm so glad that I found Bells and everything here."

"Here's the thing. I've made no secret of the fact that I am being very picky about who I sell this bookstore to. This is my life's work, and I would not be able to enjoy retirement if I thought it was in danger. I need to know that whoever takes it over will respect what Something Worth Reading is while also supporting it to continue to be successful in the long run."

"Of course."

She pointed at him. "And you said something really interesting last night."

"I did?"

She nodded. "You said that the bookstore you visited as a child felt magical and that you were glad that kids hadn't given up on that kind of magic. I don't think you were really talking to me when you said it. I think you were just reflecting. But that's exactly what I wanted to hear. That's the spirit I wanted in the next person who took this over. My goal was to create magic for everyone, to show them how magical storytelling can be. Something Worth Reading has had its own story over the decades. I want you to write the next chapter."

It took a moment for Michael to realize what she was saying. "Do you mean—"

She smiled and jutted out her hand for a handshake. "I want to sell the bookstore to you. If you still want it, of course."

He accepted the handshake, but he still felt like he was in a haze. "I definitely do. Thank you so much, Naomi."

"I was pretty sure you were the right guy the day you offered to buy it. You were so honest about what you wanted even if you weren't quite sure of it. I've got a good sense for people, and I'm not often wrong."

"Thanks, but they haven't even announced the winner of Deck the Shops yet."

"When I saw the event last night, I was confident that I was going to say yes to you, but listening to what you had to say last night and this morning sealed the deal for me. It doesn't matter if you win or not. I told you to treat this place as your own, and you did, with all of the passion and fervor I could ask for."

Michael felt his eyes stinging a little from emotion. He'd never felt this strongly about anything. When he had quit Rothstein, it was because he was angry and felt undervalued, but he didn't really care about Rothstein. He cared about Something Worth Reading, and that was a really nice feeling.

Michael could have shouted with excitement. He had gotten exactly what he had wanted.

But something struck him: he hadn't exactly gotten everything. He still wanted Emily. He wondered what would happen now if he won Deck the Shops and she didn't. Michael had wanted to win this contest because he thought it was his only path to getting the bookstore, but Emily had more personal, more sentimental reasons for wanting to win. This meant more to her than it ever really had to him. He could only hope now that she would win Deck the Shops. He wanted that for her.

"You still have your key, right?" Naomi asked, and he nodded. "Hang on to it. I have to go pack. I'll have the documents sent over to you after Christmas. You can run whatever hours you want here until I get back in January."

"You have no idea what this means to me."

She smiled. "I think I do. Merry Christmas, Michael."

"Merry Christmas."

29

Emily

The air was crisp, chillier than Emily would have preferred, but that was honestly perfect for the town's Christmas festival, the final Christmas event for Bells each year. She always hated the years that there was no snow at Christmas, so she was glad to see a few flurries already floating in the air. She pulled her coat tighter around her, tightening her scarf. She decided that she would need hot cocoa to get through the cold night, so she headed in the direction of the booth.

It was pretty much impossible for Emily to picture Christmas without picturing Bells. Her childhood in Bells was so integral to her concept of what Christmas is and should be that she genuinely didn't know how she would even celebrate Christmas in another place. Her parents had once booked a skiing trip in Colorado over Christmas break, and while she'd had a blast and Colorado was beautiful, she had missed the Christmas traditions and rituals in Bells. She had made her parents promise that they would book those kinds of trips around the Bells Christmas events from then on.

Every year, she knew exactly what her Christmas would look like, and while some people might find that boring and monotonous, she never had. It was comforting knowing that everything was always the same. She liked the familiarity of knowing everyone and getting to do the same things every year. Even most of the Deck the Shops events were the same every year.

The one thing about this year that had been different was Michael. At first, Emily had fought that. She hadn't wanted to let him in because with change there was always the risk of disappointment, of failure, of heartbreak. Trusting someone new, allowing them into your life and letting them become a big part of it, brings with it inherent risk. Emily had used to like to play it safe, but the last few weeks had taught her to push herself a little more. Her innovative ideas for Sweet Treats had been popular with customers and her grandparents. She had learned to think outside of the box.

And Michael—he had changed her life for the better. Despite her best efforts to put up walls, he had won her heart, and she was so glad for it. He was staying in Bells, hopefully he would win Deck the Shops and the bookstore, and she was so glad for all of it. She desperately wanted to see him today, to talk to him and work through the way she had panicked and shut him out. He wasn't Noah—he never had been—and it was time that she started letting him in.

She had finally reached the hot cocoa stand, but before she could get in line to order, someone held out a cup in front of her. She looked over to see Michael smiling at her, holding two cups, equally piled high with whipped cream, marshmallows, sprinkles, and a peppermint stick in each.

"I thought I'd run into you here," Michael said.

"Oh no, am I that predictable?" she said as she took a cup from him.

"I just know you that well."

Emily felt warm from more than just the hot cocoa in her hands. The way that Michael looked at her, smiled at her, made her happier than anything else. He looked at her as if she brought him great joy, like he never wanted to look at anyone or anything else. It was intoxicating to have someone look at her that way.

She pointed at his own cup of cocoa. "It looks like I've rubbed off on you. Are those toppings I see?"

He laughed and rolled his eyes. "Fine, yes, you converted me. But I'm still not insane. I'm not going to pile everything on it. I still want to taste the chocolate, you know."

"Coward."

"Mind if I walk with you for a while?"

"Not at all."

They started kind of wandering through the town square, browsing as they went. The feeling of deja vu that Emily had was not unwelcome—this was very reminiscent of the day they had walked around together at the tree lighting. Emily had found Michael so easy to talk to, his company never unwanted. The tree lighting had been the day she had decided to let down the walls a little, to let herself enjoy Michael's company, but then she had found out he was entering Deck the Shops, and she had shot those walls right back up. Winning had become the most important thing in the world to her, but things had changed.

"So, what else goes on here besides hot chocolate and announcing the Deck the Shops winner?"

"Honestly, it's basically the same thing as the tree lighting event. All the same booths come back out. There will be some Christmas caroling later, but people just hang out."

"It's nice," he said with a smile. "So, how do you feel about Deck the Shops?"

"I feel really good about how my event went," she said, and it was true. She was proud of what she had accomplished. Winning just wasn't most important anymore.

"You should be. It was really good."

"Thanks. And guess what?" she asked, and Michael raised his eyebrows. "I had a really good talk with my grandparents."

"Oh yeah?"

She nodded. "They were really impressed. We had an honest conversation about everything. They want me to take more ownership of Sweet Treats."

"That's fantastic."

"They're ready to move toward retirement, so they're officially passing the baton to me. They said they are really excited to see what I'll do to keep Sweet Treats innovative but still traditional."

"Oh, I'm sure you'll make them proud. They know how much that place means to you."

"You want to know the craziest thing? I thought for sure that I would have to win Deck the Shops to prove myself, but they said it doesn't even matter if I win. They saw the vision, and they trust me to execute it."

Michael stopped walking. "You're kidding."

She shook her head. "I just wanted to tell you that I got really caught up in beating you in Deck the Shops and winning, and when my grandparents told me that it didn't matter if I won—I don't know, I guess it made me realize that I had been focusing on the wrong thing."

"It wasn't really the wrong thing. You care a lot about the bakery and your grandparents, and there's nothing wrong with that."

"Yeah, but I got so competitive and absorbed with winning. I took it too far. It doesn't matter now. Actually, I really hope you win. I know how badly you want Something Worth Reading."

"Uh, about that. I talked to Naomi yesterday."

"How'd she like the event? It seemed like it went really well."

"It did, and she loved it. She told me that she was testing to make sure that I really wanted the bookstore for the right reasons. I didn't really know what she meant by that weeks ago, but she said I had proven that I had the right mindset."

"That's great," Emily said, and Michael laughed. "What's so funny?"

"She said I never needed to win Deck the Shops. She just wanted to see what I would do with it. She was happy with what she saw. She's selling me the bookstore."

"Oh my gosh, really? I'm so happy for you."

Emily threw her arms around his neck somewhat impulsively, but she was genuinely so happy for him that it had just been a reflex. He certainly didn't reject it; in fact, he wrapped his arms around her waist and pulled her closer to him. She smelled that cologne again and enjoyed the feeling of his arms reaching all the way around her, holding firmly, as if he were afraid that she would let go. She had no intentions of doing so.

Michael laughed softly, tousling her hair a little where his face rested against her head. "I spent all day yesterday hoping you would win Deck the Shops since I didn't need to win anymore."

Emily leaned only her head back so she could make eye contact, but she made no effort to move away from him. "I did the same thing."

"You know, my event never would have been what it was without you. You brought a spark and a magic to it. Thank you for that."

"You did the same for me. My event had no organization, and I was going in too many directions, trying too hard. You helped me rein it in."

"You didn't just bring a spark to the bookstore," he said, gazing into her eyes. "You brought a spark into my life, a spark I didn't know I was missing. Every day I've spent with you has been so bright because of the light you bring to everything you do."

"I didn't realize how much I was forcing everything in my life, trying too hard to make it exactly what I wanted or trying too hard to avoid disappointment. I'm so glad you helped me let go."

"I didn't know what I was missing until I met you," Michael said, tucking a piece of hair behind her ear that had blown out in the wind.

"Me either. And I'm sorry I blew up at you over the Rothstein offer. I jumped to a conclusion without hearing you out."

"I'm sorry I didn't talk to you about it. I didn't want to give you the impression that I was even considering it, but that's how I gave you that impression."

Emily shrugged. "It doesn't matter anymore."

"I'm just glad I'm here with you."

With that, Michael leaned in, resting a hand on Emily's jawline, and kissed her. This kiss was nothing like the kiss at the hockey game. That kiss had been quick and polite, sweet, but Emily had been suppressing her feelings back then. She was trying to fight the way she knew she felt about Michael. That was over now. She had fallen for Michael, and she was no longer interested in pretending she wasn't. This kiss was slow and intimate. No one was watching this time, and it was clear that Michael wanted to take his time. He moved both hands up to her face, cradling her chin, and Emily kept her hands on his shoulders, brushing against the edge of his hairline on his neck. Kissing Michael was at once thrilling and exciting but also familiar, as if she had been kissing Michael for years. Perhaps she was just meant to.

Emily didn't keep track of time, but after a while, they slowly let themselves separate, though Michael kept his hands gently resting on her jaw and neck. He seemed as if he wanted to say something or maybe kiss her again, but his eyes flicked up over her shoulder, and when Emily turned, she saw Renee and Darren holding each other's hands, smiling wide.

Michael smiled. "Oh, I'm never going to hear the end of this."

Emily said, "I don't think I am either."

"I guess that's what we get for kissing in the middle of the town square."

"Oh, I don't know. We also kissed on the jumbotron."

Michael laughed and kissed her on the forehead as Renee and Darren walked over.

Darren said, "Looks like you worked it out."

"I'm so happy for you both," Renee added.

"I don't mean to rush you two," Darren said, "but they're about to announce the winner of Deck the Shops. Aren't you both dying to know who won?"

Michael looked at Emily, and they both shrugged. Emily said, "I guess so."

Michael wrapped his arms around Emily's waist. "I already got what I wanted."

"Well, *I* want to know," Darren said, taking his wife's hand. "Let's go."

They gathered around the makeshift stage in the center of town just under the big tree. This was where Emily felt most at home: surrounded by everyone in this town that she loved so much.

Mayor Rayburn took the stage and stepped up to the mic. "Good evening everyone. It's lovely to see all of you here celebrating this wonderful season. We'll get on to the festivities right after this, but I know everyone is excited to hear who won Deck the Shops this year. I have to say, this was a very interesting year of entries. We saw some familiar entries, but we also saw some new things, which is so much fun."

Michael squeezed Emily's hand. "Still don't care who wins?"

Emily smiled up at him. "Not at all."

Mayor Rayburn continued: "This year was the highest voter turnout we've ever seen, and that had a very interesting impact on the outcome. For the first time in the history of Deck the Shops, we had a tie." Everyone gasped, looking around at each other and murmuring. "We tripled checked the vote count because it was so surprising, but we do indeed have a tie. So congratulations to our two winning businesses Sweet Treats and Something Worth Reading!"

The crowd erupted into cheers, and Michael and Emily looked at each other in shock. Emily could hardly believe it. She hadn't even considered that a tie would be possible. Mayor Rayburn gestured for both of them to come up to the stage to accept the trophy, so Michael took her hand, and they walked up together.

Emily had a sense of being in a blur. Everything simultaneously felt like it was in slow motion but also going so fast. First, they had both been so determined to win. Then, they were both hoping for the other to win. Then, they didn't care who would win. Both of them winning hadn't been an option, so Emily thought.

Mayor Rayburn held out the trophy, so both Michael and Emily took it, holding it between the two of them. The crowd cheered for them. She had one hand on the trophy, one hand in Michael's, and snow was falling all around them. This was a surreal moment, one Emily was certain she would remember forever.

Michael took the opportunity to lean in and kiss her, eliciting more cheers from the crowd.

He leaned in and said, "Looks like we won anyway because of each other."

"I guess we really are better together."

30

Michael

Michael passed out some gift boxes to Emily, Frank, and Eleanor, hastily wrapped by him the night before. They looked a little silly under Frank and Eleanor's tree next to their immaculately wrapped gifts, but he was happy to see them there nonetheless.

"Michael," Eleanor said, "you didn't have to get us anything."

"It was the least I could do after all of the kindness you showed me the past few weeks. Thank you for letting me crash all of your Christmas family traditions."

"You're always welcome."

"Go ahead and open them."

Eleanor and Frank unwrapped their boxes, revealing matching dancing Santa sweaters. They both laughed heartily.

"If you press the button at the bottom," Michael added, "they light up and play 'Jingle Bells.'"

They both pressed them, eliciting a mismatched tinkling, metallic rendition of the Christmas tune.

"Thanks, Michael. They're lovely."

Frank added, "But you can't borrow mine next year. You're going to have to get your own."

Emily got up and grabbed a bag from under the tree and handed it to Michael. "Then I guess you should open this now."

"You're kidding," he said, pulling out tissue paper to reveal a green sweater covered in tinsel, decorated like a gaudy Christmas tree.

"Haven't you learned by now that we *never* kid about Christmas in Bells?"

"I'm starting to." He pulled the sweater on and laughed at the tinsel sticking up everywhere. "How's it look?"

Frank laughed. "Hideous."

"Perfect."

"So," Eleanor said, "have you settled on a place?"

Michael nodded. "I'm going to take the one with the lake in the back. I'm really looking forward to getting the keys so I can start moving some stuff in."

"Will you be going back to Chicago to pack your things?"

Another nod. "In a few days. It won't take long. I never really decorated my apartment." He turned to Emily. "Any chance you'd like to come with me? I could take you out for pizza."

"Chicago style? Ugh," she said, and Michael elbowed her. "You know I'm not a city person, but I think it'll be fun with you."

"I'll do anything as long as I'm with you."

He kissed her forehead, and as Frank got up to pour more coffee and Eleanor grabbed another gingerbread cookie, he marveled at what his life had become. Just a few weeks ago, he had been working a job that was making him exhausted with no one in his life. Now, he had reconnected with Darren and was spending Christmas with the most beautiful, wonderful girl he had ever seen and her family that made Christmas feel magical, the way it always looked in the movies. He couldn't believe that he had gotten this lucky. Oddly, he found himself grateful that he had lost that promotion; it had prompted him to quit and visit Bells, and that was a decision he'd be eternally glad he had made.

Michael handed Emily a small gift box. "Open that one."

Emily pulled at the ribbon until it came off, and when she opened the box to reveal the silver Christmas wreath necklace he'd picked out a few days ago, she smiled wide.

"It's beautiful," she said.

"You liked the wreath I made, so I thought I'd get you a nicer one. Plus, you strike me as the type that wears Christmas jewelry year round."

"Uh, yes, with pride, thank you." She held it out to him. "Can you put it on?"

Eleanor followed Frank into the kitchen, winking at Michael as she passed by, leaving them alone sitting on the floor in the living room. He took the necklace clasp in his hands and fiddled with it until it opened. Emily held up her hair, and as he clipped the necklace on her, he couldn't help but soak in the moment. This was the kind of Christmas morning he had always dreamed of as a child: sitting on the floor in a Christmas sweater (albeit an ugly one) in front of a roaring fire, opening gifts with grandparent figures, eating cookies and drinking coffee, and listening to the carols playing in the background. The moment was perfect. A part of it still felt unreal to him, but he was loving every minute.

"You know," he said, "it's pretty funny that we ended up tying in Deck the Shops. I didn't even know that was a possibility."

"I didn't either."

"But I'm pretty sure we can't bet on that again."

"Probably not."

He reclined, stretching out his arm behind her. "So one us has to win next year."

"I guess so."

Michael smiled. "I'm looking forward to competing with you, then."

"As long as we get to do it together."

Michael leaned in and kissed her gently. He was so looking forward to a lifetime of Christmases just like this one.

* * *

Acknowledgements

This book was a dream of mine to write for many years. The Christmas season is my favorite time of the year. I'm the kind of person who listens to Christmas music and watches Christmas movies year round. I always wanted to write a Christmas romance, and when Emily's and Michael's stories came to me, I knew this was the perfect idea.

Thank you to Emily from LoveLitDesign for creating the most beautiful Christmas cover I've ever seen. When I first saw it, I couldn't stop staring at it, and I literally did not ask her to change a single thing from the first draft she sent me. She just nailed it immediately. It's one of my favorite book covers that I've ever seen, and I can't believe it's for a story that I wrote.

Thank you to friends who are always willing to hear my rambly thoughts, look at cover drafts, help me fix plot holes, and reassure me that I do know how to write books. Kayla Tirrell, Laina Strickland, Morgan Brownlee, Kristen Christensen, Kelly Layne: I am so thankful for our friendship and your support. It means the world to me. Thank you to Reese Overholt for being willing to read an early draft of this story to make sure Michael's point of view sounded authentic and for providing detailed feedback. I so appreciate your insight and that you did not judge me for some really dumb mistakes early on.

Thank you to my parents Brian and Sylvia with whom I watch pretty much every Christmas movie. My Christmases as a child were magical. As someone born in December, I can attest that most people born that close to

Christmas grow up either loving it or hating it, and while I'd like to think that my personality has something to do with it, I also know that it was you two who instilled a love of Christmas in me. Thank you to my sister Ashley for keeping up the Santa illusion for years after I knew the truth because I never told you. Even though I thought you still believed in Santa despite being more than seven years older than me, when I got older, I appreciated the effort you put in to keeping Christmas exciting for me.

About the author

When she's not writing books about Christmas, she's watching Hallmark Christmas movies. An English teacher in Florida, Kristen Grafton is a Florida native with an MFA in Popular Fiction & Publishing and an MA in English Rhetoric. She was a triple major in college. She has an unhealthy obsession with her cats and Taylor Swift. She is the author of *Ten Years from Now*. She is also the author of the following YA novels:

Thank You for Applying
Line of Succession
The Waves at My Window

To learn more about Kristen Grafton, follow her on Instagram @kmgrafton1 and visit www.kristenmgrafton.com.